TALES TOLD TO JOHN WILLY

By George Mitchell

For Emily, George and Tyler

Copyright © 2017 George Mitchell
Cover design S J Mitchell
All rights reserved.

No part of this book may be reproduced in any form by any electronic or mechanical means, including information or storage retrieval systems, without permission in writing from the author. The only exception is by a reviewer who may quote short excerpts in a review.

For Michaela with best wishes, George.

These stories are entirely works of fiction. The names, characters and incidents portrayed are the work of the author's imagination. Any resemblance to actual persons, living or dead is entirely coincidental.

CONTENTS

THE ARMISTEADS   5

GIANT   20

GONE   32

ROBOT, OR JANE THE TERRIBLE, OR SOUND   47

BIRD OF THE DESERT   70

UTHER   90

CONTACT   106

MAYA   131

WALKABOUT   147

THE ARMISTEADS

Our family is not as big as it seems. People sometimes ask me how many Armisteads there are because, besides ourselves, we have relatives and friends who visit us regularly and often stay in our house. I think they enjoy our company. Not only do we as a family enjoy having friends around but there is always a plentiful supply of good food. We have spare space in our rambling old house so that people can stay with us and there is often something happening, perhaps someone's new venture is being discussed, or maybe an impromptu dance/singing/music session, or an interesting argument, or a game being played that anyone can join in. For example; the ping pong ball challenge, which involves stuffing a ping pong ball into your mouth and then expressing it with as big a breath as you can muster. The resulting distance gained is meticulously measured by Dad. At the moment the champion distance is four metres and thirteen centimetres gained by Zachary, although there was some discussion as to whether or not an open window in one of the bathrooms had caused a momentary wind advantage but, after some investigation, the record was accepted. At other times we might simply enjoy getting together in one of big downstairs rooms to talk about our lives and interests and sometimes offer support to any one of us who might be having a problem.

In our immediate family, we have a

range of ages, starting with me, Michael. I'm fourteen and trying desperately to get older. I have dark hair like Mum but generally, it seems that I am average: average height, average looks and average at school. Next is my brother Joshua, he's fifteen. He has fair hair like Dad and he is good looking, and clever. Mostly I hate him although when we play football together we seem to have an intuitive understanding of where the other one is on the field and are able to pass the ball to one another without looking. This makes us successful and popular in the 'B team'. Outside football, however, we have as little to do with one other as possible, particularly in our social life: he has a girlfriend and I have spots. Despite our differences, however, we still have the family ethic, instilled into all of us from an early age, that in a crisis, we will support one another regardless of the situation. After me and my brother, is Daisy, who is sixteen. She is dark like me but also clever, kind and pretty, has lots of friends and generally loves to help people. Mum says she'll end up working for a charity. I'm not sure about that because Daisy has always had an incredible imagination. She makes up wonderful stories to the point where we aren't always sure whether she's telling the truth or inventing. Mum calls it 'romancing'. When we were small I loved it when Daisy told me bedtime stories. They were better than those in books and her lovely quiet voice made everything seem safe when she talked. I wasn't alone in this; we all loved her to tell us a story especially at birthdays and Christmas when she would make up special ones for the occasion. So I think that Daisy could end up writing books fuelled by her wonderful imagination.

Then there's Zachary, who is over six feet tall and has decided to wear his hair very short so that he can use his electric cutters to keep it tidy. Recently he is trying to grow a beard but it's coming out stripy fair and dark. We don't see much of him because he's at University doing something scientific and unpronounceable. He regards himself as superior, being the first Armistead to be involved in further education. We see him and his girlfriend during holidays and sometimes at weekends. He has developed a student drawl and uses words like 'cool' for anything he likes and 'gross' for other things like younger brothers, me in particular. I like his girlfriend. She's called Hermione and is tall, classically beautiful and kind. She smiles at me and sometimes gives me a cuddle. I am in love. She is far too good for Zack and I dream of whisking her off when she finally realises that it's me she loves.

The eldest is Christine. She looks like Mum's younger sister. She is twenty three and my favourite sibling. She gives me a big hug every day and whispers that I'm her favourite but not to tell the others. (I actually think it's because I'm the youngest). Her fiancé is Bob; he's ace. He rides a huge, powerful motorbike and works as a car mechanic. Dad likes him because he can repair our aging family people carrier, which has done well over 100,000 miles but is big enough to accommodate us all when

8

required, including the final member of our family: Grandpa John Willy. Grandpa still has plenty hair which is completely white. I like his hands. They're brown and covered with wrinkles and seem to be just right for him, as though they've lived a life and done a lot of things. He says that he is as old as his teeth but since he hasn't got any, this is not useful information. He is Mum's dad. She says he is eighty-three but he says that nobody really knows.

Grandpa also tells us that he used to be over six feet tall but that the cares of a challenging life have worn him down to his present five feet seven inches. He has travelled a lot and worked in different countries, so he has lots of tales to tell. Mum says that most of them are true but she's not always sure because some of his adventures happened before she was born but she does remember living in Hong Kong when he worked there as a policeman. They sometimes speak Cantonese to one another which, to me, sounds as if they're having an argument.

'Grandpa's like our Daisy,' says Dad. 'You're never quite sure whether he's telling the truth or not.'

'All absolutely true,' Grandpa bridles. 'Would I tell you a lie?' He says but with a wink from a wrinkled eye, so we're never quite sure.

You need to know that we all love Grandpa. He pretends to be tough and often curses politicians and others in high office because he says they don't really care about ordinary people and are all out for themselves but within our family, he is kind and generous. Anyone with a problem will get support from him; whether it is just a kind word or advice or even some money to help them acquire a longed-for item. All of us, even the adults, will have been thankful for his support at sometime in their lives.

If he has a problem, however, nobody knows because he keeps it to himself, like when he was having a lot of pain, particularly when climbing stairs. He struggled on without complaining until one day Mum found him sitting halfway up the first flight, unable to get any further, with tears in his eyes because of the pain. When questioned, he said he'd felt a bit dizzy but would be fine with a minute's rest. It was ages before he would admit that the problem was his right hip but he said he didn't want any fuss, he could 'manage', which was his favourite phrase.

'Don't trust doctors,' he said. 'Hate hospitals; they didn't do any good for Elsie, why would they do any good for me?'

'It's because Grandma died in hospital,' Mum told us. 'He still misses her and can't forgive them for not making her better.'

In the end after much cajoling from us and his friend Geoffrey telling him how much better he was walking with a replacement hip, Grandpa agreed to go and have his done but continued to argue that he could have 'managed' if we'd left him alone. He was, of course, much better and, although he has to use a stick, now manages stairs without difficulty.

For several years after this crisis, Grandpa John Willy returned to being our kind and cheerful friend but he was getting gradually older and, a few months ago, his coughing, particularly at night, became a bit of a worry. He never complained, however, and although Mum tried to question him about it he just told her not to fuss, he was fine. He did eventually agree to see the doctor and was given a range of inhalers which definitely helped to improve his breathing, although he still had the occasional cough that seemed come from deep within his chest. Despite his increasing years, he never stopped helping us and taking an interest in our troubles and triumphs.

As with all families, we experienced troubles but generally the life of the family rumbled on. Everybody was busy with work or school or leisure activities so, while in the back of our minds we were aware that Grandpa's coughing formed a background accompaniment to life, he never complained, consequently; we didn't worry about him. I recalled afterwards that whenever we were looking for him someone would say, 'he's gone to the toilet', even when he wasn't in there. It became a standard family joke.

His uncomplaining attitude and our generally busy lives meant that we were not really as sensitive to his situation as we should have been. We were very surprised, therefore, when one day, to our general dismay, Grandpa John Willy called us all together and made an announcement. He told us, quite calmly, that while he loved us all, he was fed up with several aspects of his life: with the lack of sleep he was experiencing; the inconvenience of his increasingly regular visits to the doctor, whenever his breathing problems flared up; the fact that his other hip was now giving him great pain and the need to be near a toilet because of the regularity of his being 'taken short'. He also said that the last thing he wanted was to become a nuisance – a burden on the family. 'Also, there is no way that I want to end up in a rest home, sitting round in those awful chairs with my head lolling down, waiting to die.'

Finally, he made it clear that he had no intention of going back to hospital again. 'They'll just mess me about and it's really just old age that's the problem. They can't do anything for me, I'm too old.'

Mum decided to speak. 'Dad, this isn't like you, you shouldn't talk like this, it's just silly, stop it now.' I could see that her eyes were wet as she spoke.

Grandpa looked sad when he replied. 'The last thing I want to do is to upset anyone, particularly you love, but I've made a decision which I think is better for me and good for this wonderful family.'

He went on to explain that he believed that he had reached an age where he could solve his problems by 'passing-on'. It was at this point that most of us, bearing in mind that the old man was notorious for his creative imagination, decided that this was in the nature of a joke so one by one we decided to laugh, until everyone joined in.

'Good one Grandpa, you had us going

then,' Dad said, rising from his chair. 'Sorry to break this up but I've got some gardening to do.' With this he left.

The rest of us were now happy that what we'd heard was another of Grandpa's tales. We couldn't see how anyone could just decide to die; we just couldn't take it seriously. Only Mum and Daisy looked glum and moved a bit closer to the old man and started talking to him.

Later, when we all gathered to eat our evening meal, we got the first evidence that the old man might be serious.

'I'll just eat enough so that I gradually subside,' he explained, pushing his still half-full plate away. 'And so that there is some pleasure in my life, I'll take a little whisky and water from time to time.' We were all aware of his love for food, evidenced by his usual willingness to eat up any leftovers, so we were a little disturbed by this.

Mum was cross. 'Dad, don't be ridiculous, the joke's gone far enough.' But he was adamant and ate no more food, which was fine by Josh and me since we got the excess.

Later on, in the evening, we found him carrying a pile of clothes and the photo albums of his travels round the world into the downstairs toilet. When questioned he explained that he had decided to live in there. 'I might as well stay there till I go,' he said, describing how he could prevent any opening of the door by wedging it with his walking stick. 'It's hardly ever used and there's nothing much in there except the toilet and shower and that old cupboard used for useless items, like old

13

toys and clothes that need to be sent to Oxfam.'

While Mum is usually tolerant of his idiosyncrasies, this was where she drew the line: 'You are not to live in there Grandpa, that's ridiculous. There's no proper bed and I need to keep the house clean, you'll just be in the way when I need to get in there. Also, while you're listening to me for once, this talk of dying is nonsense. You're not going to die. For one thing the doctor says you're still fit for your age and, so long as we look after you, you've got years of life left.'

Lowering himself onto the hall chair, Grandpa replied. 'That's just it, you'll have to look after me. I don't want to be looked after! You've enough to do without looking after me.'

Hearing the voices, everyone had gathered to find out what was going on and Daisy began to cry. 'I don't want you to die Grandpa,' she wailed.

Mum looked stern, 'Now look what you've done you silly old man. Just stop this nonsense.'

But he was determined. 'I'm sorry Daisy but it's no fun getting old and decrepit and you young folks have got your own lives to live without looking after me.'

Now, there was a general clamour, with everyone talking at once, until Dad raised his voice. 'Enough, enough, we'll not get anywhere with everyone talking at once. Let's speak one at a time. We have to understand Grandpa's point of view. He's fed up with hospital visits and feeling dependent on us. He's always been an independent man who has looked after others, especially the family and he feels that he can't do this any more and hates it. Right, John Willy?'

'Yes Harry, that's it. But I don't want anyone to be upset, particularly Daisy. Now I'm upset because she's upset and I don't know what to do.'

Christine spoke for the first time. 'Grandpa, maybe if you think about what bits of life you enjoy, you know, what makes life worth living? Perhaps that will help to change your mind.'

'Yes, you like Match of the Day,' suggested Joshua. 'You like shouting at the tele when players make mistakes.'

'Load of fairies they are these days, rolling on the floor screaming when they've been tickled. In my day …,' here, he paused, realising that for a moment he had forgotten his plan.

'And you like my food,' offered Mum. The old man nodded.

'And reading the paper,' I suggested.

'And I'll keep telling you stories,' Daisy's quiet voice, still tearful, cut through the tension, making everyone feel calmer.

Grandpa looked at her. 'You know Daisy; I think your stories are one of the best things in my life.'

Daisy smiled at this and, wiping away the remnants of a tear, walked over to him, sat on his knee and gave his wrinkled cheek a kiss. 'I'll tell you my stories every time I think of a new one if you stop talking about dying.'

So, there it was, simple as it seems,

Christine's prompting, the combination of suggestions about food, football and newspapers but mainly Daisy's stories, were enough to make Grandpa consider changing the plans for his demise.

'Maybe once a week?' He suggested, a bit sheepishly.

'No problem,' smiled Daisy, pleased that she had helped find an answer to a family problem. He did insist, however, in keeping one aspect of his plan: the downstairs toilet was to be his to visit at a moment's notice whenever required.

'I don't want to inconvenience anyone, but it's just terrible when I arrive at the door in urgent need and find someone else in there.'

*

Fortunately, as the young people in the family got older and were no longer prepared to share bedrooms, our family had had to move into Green Hedges; a detached Victorian pile, surrounded on all sides by gardens consisting mainly of grassed areas with dusty, privet hedges providing an effective border that didn't need too much pruning. The house had three floors plus a large attic. There was a large kitchen, a dining room that can only be described as palatial, and two other ground floor rooms, one big enough to accommodate us all for family activities and the other a small sitting room where Grandpa spent a lot of time because it was warm, had a tele, two comfortable chairs and was near the toilet. (I wonder if the big room is what estate agents would describe as a 'reception' room, intended for posh people to greet important guests in evening dress.) If so ours was not a reception room, just a space for our eccentric family, where they could argue, laugh, watch tele, fight, sulk, play games, sing, play musical instruments (badly), have parties, fart silently (most people), fart loudly (Grandpa), drink, eat takeaways, share secrets, weep together, discuss: problems, finance, politics, sport, girl friends and boy friends; in other words, any activity that could be performed with others. Anything that required privacy, such as snogging, (Christine and sometimes Zachary), studying, sleeping, reading and weeping alone had to be done upstairs in one of the bedrooms, although this did not prevent interruption, particularly when it came to snogging, because our young family members delighted in feigning surprise when barging in on a romantic interlude.

    The gloomy, oak panelled entrance hall opened on to a wide staircase which led to a first floor with four bedrooms. Above that, the second floor had the same number and a winding, wrought iron spiral staircase carried anyone interested to the attic which, at some time, had been split into several small rooms with sloping roof lights for daytime illumination. There was also one small bathroom/toilet in the attic. It was generally agreed that these rooms had, at one time, been used to house domestic staff. During the period of our living in the house, they held only dust, spiders, birds' nests and family 'stuff' that was either past usefulness or discarded for the moment.

In the current circumstance of John Willy's reclusive activities, the existence of spacious bathrooms on both upper floors meant that the rest of the family was not unduly 'inconvenienced'. It simply meant that guests were asked to use the upstairs toilets when required and the family, particularly the males, were asked to ensure that unwashed under garments were placed in the laundry basket and not left where they might cause offence. That is not to say that the females were necessarily tidy in this matter but small flimsies, changed regularly, were less likely to present an odorous problem for visitors than those worn by males who might occasionally retain underpants beyond their 'wash by' date.

During this period, as the youngest family member, I was keen to get through my teenage years, trying to arrive at manhood as quickly as possible. It was increasingly tiresome to be told, 'oh it's your age love; you'll grow out of it.' The 'it' in question seemed to be any suggestion of an opinion, or attempt to exercise an individual choice or decision that was out of place with what my seniors considered to be 'normal'. Consequently, I wanted to be twenty because I imagined that people might then consider it inappropriate to offer the same level of paternalistic advice. (In the end this proved not to be the case since, even when I achieved my goal, everyone in the family was older than me and still considered that I had not yet grown up). Despite my desires, however, time limped along with infuriating slowness

But I must not digress into my personal issues; let's get back to the problem of Grandpa John Willy's request. Although, for a few days, his desire to remain in or near to the downstairs toilet did not create any significant problems, in fact most of us were happy to manage without his critical comments on our dress, hair, friends or activities, an issue did arise at the weekly 'story time' because we all enjoyed Daisy's stories and didn't want to miss hearing them. Eventually, after much pleading and bribery, we persuaded John Willy to join us in the big 'reception' room once a week so that everyone could listen to Daisy's calm, delightful delivery.

She was really good at making her tales relevant to an individual. She knew that Grandpa had been in the army and travelled to many countries. He'd also had lots of different jobs, including being a policeman and, at one time, had worked as an interior decorator.

At the end of the first week then, there we all were, gathered together and ready to hear the first of Daisy's stories for Grandpa John Willy. It had been decided that Saturday, late afternoon was a good time. The football scores were in, Zachary could be home from Uni to see Hermione and Christine and Bob would be in before going out for the evening. Since you know a bit about our family now, I thought you might like to hear the story.

The first one was about China. During his time working for the police force in Hong

Kong, Grandpa sometimes ventured into the mainland and even went as far as the Great Wall. Daisy decided that this was a good place to start. After Joshua and I had been separated to prevent us from fighting and Mum had fetched some sewing, Daisy, reading from word-processed sheets in her usual quiet voice, began: 'I'm pretending that I'm the young man in the story, hope you like it, I call it:

GIANT

Morning; the Great Wall was touched by low, winter sunshine. A dark shadow fell on the west side covering ground hardened by frost. On the eastern side the old stone glowed through the black branches of bare trees. The ancient pile snaked away into the distance, writhing round hilltops, and plummeting into hidden valleys. The sky was ice blue and a thin arctic breeze tried to penetrate my heavy woollen jacket. I pushed my hands deeper into the pockets and pulled the coat tight to my chest. Chilled, an involuntary shudder went through my body but I rejoiced in the beauty of the day. Tourists gathered near the entry point, amazed at the spectacle but too cold or nervous to wander far. They marvelled at the spectacle, took photographs, but were now unsure what to do. They had travelled thousands of miles to be here and wanted to celebrate their arrival but what can you do on a wall? It stretched into the far distance and had no end. If it had been a castle wall, they would have walked around and ended where they began. But this wall was different, where did it go? It went nowhere, maybe to infinity. To walk along would simply have meant retracing their steps at some point, and to minds programmed to consider the cost-efficiency of everything, such activity was pointless. Yet here they were; a famous monument, created by countless, long dead, human beings, hundreds of years ago, lay before them. I could sense the tourists' frustration. You can look, take photographs, say to others how marvellous it is and then what? To simply walk back down the hill, buy some souvenirs and get on the coach, seemed inadequate but there was nothing else to do.I determined to leave them behind before I was infected by their mood. I would go as far as possible and then return or simply get off at a convenient point. In any case, I was cold, and the exercise would warm me up. My taxi might wait or the driver could leave with another fare – it didn't matter. I was an adult and I would cope, whatever happened.

Relieved to move away from the crowd, I became energised by the cold clarity of the spectacle – distant hills and valleys rose and fell, seeming to come closer to show their beauty - only falling away as I acknowledged their splendour. After initial easy walking, the next stretch went sharply uphill; steep, narrow steps, so narrow that they had to be negotiated by turning sideways. Then a long flat section led to the nearest sentry tower where a dark doorway led into a small 'castle' with cramped rooms. A tiny, wizened woman, sitting in a corner out of the wind, held out her hand, showed me two silver coins but said nothing. I shook my head but she nodded and thrust the coins towards me. I almost turned to go, but for some reason, hesitated and pulled a note from my pocket, without looking at the value. With one quick movement, she took the note, pushed the coins into my palm and, with amazing speed, proceeded to hobble off along the way I had come. The coins were warm in my hand and were covered with Chinese characters. They looked old but I suspected that they were worthless. I had fallen into a tourist trap.

On the other side of the sentry post, the wall swept steeply downhill with steps that this time, fortunately, were broad enough to accommodate the whole width of my feet. Eyes down, I descended, seeing only the grey stone, stained and worn in places but secure, immovable. I could sense hordes of dim figures clad in grey padded clothes, carrying ancient weapons and jostling against my shoulders. We walked together – dead colleagues on either side.

The slope gradually levelled out to become a flat section. Breathing was easier, the army melted away. To the east the sun was higher but still low enough to blind me for an instant. Pausing to look over the wall, to the left

I could see the small figures of tourists standing, gazing but motionless, no-one followed. I felt pleasure and fear in my isolation. Ahead, the wall rose gradually up a hillside and then twisted and disappeared. If I continued I would probably be out of sight but there should be no stopping, which would be cowardice. What could happen? I would simply be alone with an ancient pile of stones and a winter morning. The wall knew everything, time was its companion. Perhaps it would enjoy my solitary feet on its back. Was it possible to have a relationship with an inanimate object? I had rejected the people behind and chosen the wall – would this please it or would it resent my intrusion into its isolation?

I climbed steadily, feeling fitter, my breathing deep and steady. The pain in my legs was pure joy. Muscles softened by modern living began to recall their purpose. They responded, tensing and relaxing with a powerful rhythm. The wall helped me along, the ancient stone floor rose and fell in a curious rhythm as my feet pressed against it. We had a shared tempo the wall and me.

Landscapes rose and fell like huge waves against the immovable stones of a massive sea wall. Wall smiled at their puny efforts – 'many have tried to break me, you can never succeed. A stone may fall but I will never be defeated, I am the eternal warrior.'

On we went. Rather than tiring, I acquired strength and stamina. Further away from the tourist area, some damage had not been repaired: occasional steps were rounded so that they became like a slope, in places sections were missing and presented a challenge to an amateur climber. On we went though. The wall showed no signs of capitulating; I had to stay with it, or our adventure would be incomplete. The rhythm of my steps changed. Carried along by the power of the stones, I could feel the wall's pleasure at our relationship. My mind was able to relax – the physical effort was now minimal. I opened my thoughts to memories. Men, who carried, carved and set the grey granite, whispered to me about the amalgam of pain and pleasure they had experienced. The man whose foot was crushed told me of his efforts to carry on with the work while leaning on a twisted crutch broken from a tree and of the cruelty of the overseer who drove him to work harder until he slipped and fell, breaking both arms. Unable to rise, he was simply abandoned to his fate as the wall grew inexorably on its serpentine journey to infinity. I too had no time to pause and listen as the rhythm of the edifice propelled me onwards. I heard him call in pain as once more he was left behind to bemoan his lonely end, the voice of the overseer in my ear: 'leave him we have no time, the wall is our master.'

    A high eagle drifted, its eyes narrow, searching. It sneered at my leaden pace – diving and skimming low along the snaking structure, mocking me and the immobile stones. She glared as she passed, then rose, careening, spilling air from her wings and rising almost out of sight. Her voice called to us. 'Fooooools …'

Wall answered, 'I will never die …'

Faintly she replied, 'you are already deeeeeaaaad …'

Wall was angry and hurried me onwards, increasing the pace. 'We shall see who is dead' it grumbled, 'I'll show you dead!'

Now I felt the pace. My heart beat increased, the steep climbs left me breathless. Perhaps it meant to kill me in revenge for the bird's mockery. We moved into a crumbling watch tower and in the corner, an old woman whined and held out two ancient looking coins. 'No food,' she cried, pointing to her toothless mouth, 'hungry, hungry.'

I paused. Was it the same woman? I thrust my hand into a pocket, in search of payment. 'Leave her, we have no time,' said Wall, driving me on. I grabbed coins and threw them towards her. The ancient coins appeared in my palm in return although the woman didn't seem to move.

As we left the tower I glanced over my shoulder to see the woman shuffling back along the wall towards the long distant tourists. I could feel Wall's anger as my pace grew even faster until I was almost running. I cried out.

'Nearly there, nearly there,' it called. 'Hurry …'

We had reached a crumbling section that soared up, seeming to reach the darkening sky. The eagle circled, watching. This was the hardest part; my legs were burning with pain, my chest ached as lungs searched for the cold air. We rose, mist wrapped around my legs, seeming to hold me back as Wall drove me on. 'Faster, keep moving.'

'You will kill me,' I gasped

'Maybe ...'

Finally we reached the top. I leaned against the surrounding stones, straining for air. As my breathing became easier, I was able to take account of my surroundings. This seemed to be a section of Wall completely unlike any other. The structure had changed from secure, hard granite to something less substantial – almost like hard-packed earth which had suffered serious erosion, with sections crumbling away as a steep slope descended towards an open plain.

The surrounding countryside looked desolate as though it had suffered a serious and prolonged drought. Bare, twisted trees rose from a desert-like ground. Dust devils twisted towards the horizon, raising columns of dust and dead leaves. Not a creature stirred.

It was not until Wall spoke, 'there, this is what you must see', that I focussed on a shape on the ground below. It seemed almost human; with mounds for a head, arms, body and legs but of such an extraordinary size that it couldn't be a person, nevertheless, looking more carefully at the head, shapes like features were clearly visible. The fact that it was the same colour as its desert surroundings made it difficult to distinguish that this shape was something separate from the rest of the flat plain. Looking more closely, the whole began to slowly emerge until I realised that this was in fact an enormous body, a giant. I gasped, unable to form a word. Before I could clarify my thoughts, Wall whispered with a voice of heart rending sadness. 'He is my friend and he is dying.' Almost instantly, the air was filled with an unearthly groan, which seemed to rise from the prone body. The sound reverberated along the dead land and echoed into the distant hills. It was a sound that froze the soul as though death itself had spoken.

'He is your friend?'

'We are giants, together for many years. I was alone for centuries but he came from the north and spoke to me. He recognised me as a living thing, not as something dead and inanimate. He is old now and dying. I too cannot live if he is gone ... help him if you can.' As the words permeated my mind, a distant section of Wall cracked, sending piles of stone, soil and mortar tumbling to the ground with an ominous roar as if the process of dying had begun.

I could have wept at the sadness in Wall's voice. The whole dry plain sighed and the clouds lowered, trying to engulf us in a damp, miserable mist. What could I do? How do you help a dying giant? I could not speak for fear of increasing the sorrow of the moment. It was as if the whole world was waiting for me to act.

I clambered down the uneven steps of packed earth, which in places were so badly eroded that they became little more than a steep slope. At one point, my feet slipped so that I began to slide downwards, increasing in speed until I simply lay on my back and allowed my body to descend, holding out my arms as rudimentary brakes. As I neared the place where the giant lay, the slope gradually lessened so that my body came to a gentle stop in a cloud of dust. I brushed myself down as best I could and found that I was standing near the huge feet which appeared to be clad in rudimentary sandals apparently made from strands of woven tree bark. Filled with trepidation, I could not help but touch the toe that protruded from the end of the primitive footwear; a little toe as big as my head! My fingers encountered a rough surface which, to my horror, crumbled under my touch. Specks of soil fell to the ground and a small hole was left in the toe where my fingers had been. A soft moan came from the giant's mouth and Wall's voice whispered, angrily. 'You cannot touch him.'

I stepped away in despair. How could I possibly help this creature, if creature it was? I was not a doctor or nurse. I had no medicines or first aid equipment No-one else was around, there were no towns nearby; I had no apparent means or understanding by which I might provide any form of succour. An ancient construction was calling upon me to effect a cure for a giant made from soil and stones that was apparently dying. This was an impossible situation. I didn't know where I was. A strange force had driven me away from other people, away from any kind of human support. I was overwhelmed by my sense of isolation, frightened by my predicament and weary to the point of exhaustion.

As if perceiving my fear and frustration, Wall spoke again, very softly and kindly this time. 'I think you should rest and help will come in a little while.' The softness of the tone of this strange voice allied to my sudden extreme fatigue combined to generate an irresistible need for sleep. Without pausing to consider the dangers, I lay down next to the giant and almost immediately experienced an extreme drowsiness begin to invade my senses and I felt myself falling ...

*

The old woman followed a path that was barely visible alongside a little visited section of the Great Wall. No-one had been this way for many years because the structure was crumbling and dangerous, having been constructed using only hard packed clay bricks. Now, however, the wall seemed to be in perfect condition. Indeed, as far as the eye could see, the structure appeared to have been renewed.

She studied the ground carefully, obviously seeking something. She knelt to the ground by a depression that looked as though it could have been left by a sleeping man. After a few moments of searching through the loose sand, the woman gave a little cry of pleasure, bending, she collected four ancient silver coins. Thrusting them into a hidden pocket of her skirt, she turned and went back the way she had come, only pausing for a moment to gaze at an enormous, much deeper depression, which lay alongside. Taking care not to wander too close its steep sides, she turned and headed back towards the wall. From a great height, an eagle cried. 'He's goooooone, gooooone.' The old woman raised a silver coin and laughed as it glistened in the frosty sunshine.'

Daisy's stopped speaking and looked around to see our reaction. For a moment no-one spoke, then Dad smiled. 'Good one Daisy, I don't know how you do it.'

'Lovely,' said Mum. 'Poor man though, I feel sorry for him.'

'What happened to him?' I was puzzled by the abrupt end but received a cushion round the head, thrown by Joshua.

'Leave him alone,' Christine frowned at him. 'Just think for a while Michael and you'll understand.'

In the end I had to ask Christine to explain it to me. Most important though, Grandpa loved it and said the story reminded him of a day when he walked the ancient wall. 'Anyone would think that you'd been there Daisy,' he said.

'I've listened to you talking about it,' she replied, smiling at the old man. 'I'm glad you liked it.'

'I did, can't wait for next week, how about another one tomorrow?'

Daisy was about to reply when Mum interrupted. 'No Dad, you made a deal, don't try to bend the rules. It's not fair to expect Daisy to produce stories like sausages. You'll have to stay alive for another week.'

'OK,' Grandpa, grinned. 'Talking of

sausages, is it teatime yet?'

Mum laughed. 'You're a wicked old man. I thought you said you would only eat a little and 'gradually subside', now you're suddenly interested in sausages.'

John Willy looked sheepish. 'Sorry, can't talk, I need to pay a call.'

The following week, Daisy arrived to find us all gathered, ready to listen, Joshua and me at opposite ends of the big sofa separated by Bob and Christine. Mum sat by the window to get the light for her sewing. Dad was in his favourite chair. Zachary and Hermione sat together in a big armchair and Grandpa had his special one with an electric control to help him get out easily. Mum had told her best friend Doreen about the story telling and she had asked if she might listen, so she sat by the window as well.

'Oh, you're all here.' Daisy looked round to see that we had left her a chair facing us all. 'So I'm to sit here then,' she said with a grin. 'I thought these stories were just for Grandpa.'

'Oh, come on Daisy,' Dad spoke. 'You know we all want to listen.'

''I know. I'm glad you like them really. Well today's is about a man who does interior decorating, like Grandpa used to do but maybe a bit different. I call it:

GONE

Some unfortunate people wallow like sludge worms in a morass of gossip, self-approbation and vindictive judgement. Such a one was Hildegard Bloom. With her friends Hortense and Penelope, she would spend hours in negative analysis of the activities and behaviour of any person, male or female who might come anywhere near to their sphere of operation. Although immediate offspring were usually exempt, spouses were given particular attention since all three ladies believed that they could have done better in the matrimonial stakes. Having clearly married beneath their stations, they enjoyed comparing their husbands' shortcomings, marvelling at the similarities that each observed, while dwelling on how much better their lives would have been had a really suitable candidate been available. It was not unknown for their parents to enter the firing line since they were responsible for pressing entirely unsuitable marriages on to their daughters. (It is possible that a grain of truth was present here since all three groups of parents were heartily glad to see the back of daughters who constantly griped that they had not had the benefits in terms of education and introductions to high society that were enjoyed by their, apparently, more fortunate friends.)

Hildegard, proud of the way in which she had created a beautiful home in the face of the lack of resources provided by George her spouse, ran the weekly tea party to which the other two were invited. Best crockery and suitable buns from Maughams the posh Bakers were acquired and at 15.00 hours every Wednesday, with the ladies' ample figures wrapped in their best apparel, the session commenced.

'Have you heard ...' was the usual opening gambit, since although to outside observers, they might be considered to be friends, there was a high level of competition between the ladies, each vying to expose a new nugget of information that could be presented for dissection and analysis. Today's subject was a regular – Betty Smith – a poor soul who had the misfortune to be happily married with two beautiful and educationally successful children. She was a sociable woman, popular and helpful, often asked to take a leading role in local matters: chairman of the 'Inner Wheel', member of the local drama group and supporter of charity events. Her husband was a doctor who worked at the town's health centre, well-liked and rumoured to be in line to head a new, larger centre in the city. In effect then, Betty was dead game for the triumvirate of vultures.

'I saw her at Tesco's on Wednesday, you'll never believe what she was wearing ...' Hildegard paused for effect, not really expecting an answer. Since she was the provider of the food and drink, the others were prepared to allow her first strike. 'A very short skirt and high heels, she looked like a ... well you know, I can't mention such a person in my house.'

'She just thinks she's still a teenager,' offered Hortense, folding her arms to emphasise the affront she was apparently feeling. 'I've seen her dressed like that before, I think it's such bad example to present before her children. How must they feel to see their mother looking like a … no, I can't say it either.'

Penelope felt it was her turn. 'Oh, I do so agree,' she crooned, 'there's a time and place for seductive dress and Tesco's in the morning, is neither. I sometimes think we should perhaps send out a leaflet offering a little fashion advice to some of our less aware neighbours.'

This notion met with complete approval from the triumvirate, who were happy to regard themselves as potential leaders of the female members of local society. The morning progressed pleasantly as the ladies discussed how their advice leaflets might be structured and which particular women would benefit. Tea and cakes were consumed and a pleasant morning sun shone through the lace curtains increasing the golden glow of satisfaction felt by the members of the wake as their criticisms of local people, particularly women, increased in venom. George hid in the garage, waiting for the signal that he was required to remove the cups and empty plates. He was quite happy to be out of the way, avoiding the stench of mendacious propaganda that seeped insidiously from the lounge.

George was a man who longed for a quiet life. He enjoyed the occasional cigarette along with a glass of whisky, neither of which were allowed inside the house, and loved to watch and read about cricket. Having played the game in his youth, he always hoped that his son Arthur would take up the game and, in George's dreams, even possibly reach county standard and turn out for his beloved Yorkshire.

The dreams never stood a chance. Before Arthur could take hold of the bat that George had bought for him, Hildegard had announced, 'ballroom dancing, that's the thing for my son. It's such a lovely thing to do. Look at those gorgeous young men on 'Come Dancing', how tall and handsome they are and such beautiful movers. How they spin their partners and lift them effortlessly into the air oh … lovely.' Her eyes glazed over as she imagined herself being carried with grace and rhythm around a spot lit dance floor by a beautifully dressed, Adonis. 'His clumsy father could never manage something like that but I'm sure my lovely son can.'

So, the die was cast, from an early age, Arthur attended Hilda Larkin's Starlight Ballroom Academy. Even when attending his weekday school, his hair was always kept tidy with a neat parting; his shoes were black-leather and polished to a high sheen (by George) and he wore a tie which created great amusement for the other children. Despite the fact that he had little sense of rhythm, hated the way he was dressed and had feet that wouldn't follow the precise patterns required by Ms Larkin, Arthur was made to attend twice during the week after school and once on Saturday mornings.

This pattern continued for several years

until eventually, as the boy reached his early teens, he could take no more and refused to go to a place he had grown to hate. A huge scene resulted with Hildegard weeping and shouting by turns until her display culminated in a threat to commit suicide if Arthur refused to obey. Unfortunately, for his mother, Arthur had grown hardened over the years having witnessed similar performances when her wishes had been thwarted, so that he simply refused to go. George was, of course ordered to discipline his son, at which point he tentatively suggested that maybe Arthur might try cricket instead but it was too late. Since his father had given him no support when the boy had privately expressed to him a desire to stop the hated dancing classes, Arthur had decided that both his parents were determined to make his life as miserable as possible and that the only solution was to go his own way.

Much to his mother's displeasure the boy joined a local go-cart club and over the years became proficient at both driving and mechanics, which eventually led on to a career as a motor mechanic and an involvement in Formula 2 racing. At this stage, he met and fell in love with Angela, one of the other mechanics on the team and they decided to join forces and live together in a mobile home that was ideal for travelling to the various venues where the racing was held. Arthur blossomed under his new found freedom and life was good.

Hildegard hated the fact that Arthur was clearly happy away from her control and loathed Angela who she saw as a rival for HER son's affections. She was, however, faced with either disowning her only son or accepting his life preferences. The latter course seemed expedient and George was not surprised when his wife expressed pride in Arthur's success in his chosen field, nor was he the least taken aback by her claim that her son's achievements were down to her encouraging advice that he should assert his independence and reject his father's suggestion of becoming involved in that stupid game.

George through years of experience, declined to protest. The outcome for his son was good: he had escaped from his mother's dominance and entered a career that had good prospects for job satisfaction and income. The fact that George was still the butt of her complaints and demands was a small price to pay for his son's happiness. He just quietly got on with his life, subjugating himself to his wife's requirements.

Since his son had left, it was decided that, because George was such an untidy person, it would be better if he kept out of the main rooms in the house until he was required, for example, to eat, sleep or use the bathroom. Hildegard thought that the garage offered a suitable place for his activities, a small, portable television, electric fire and folding camp chair offered sufficient comfort for a man with few needs and here he would be able to smoke his 'disgusting' cigarettes and, unknown to her, have the occasional small glass of whisky. A small electric buzzer was fitted so that his required presence in the house could be indicated.

Today, as it summoned him to remove the tea things, George wondered about the quality of his life. Arthur had escaped, why couldn't he? But where would he go? He had no friends - Hildegard didn't encourage male company, regarding all men as lesser beings, - his relatives were all dead and his wife controlled the couples' respective pensions and all income and expenditure. I might as well not exist, he thought. He paused in rising from his camping chair, appalled at this terrible thought, and stood, for a moment frozen, horrified. A long, clearly annoyed repeat of the buzzing broke his reverie and he dismissed the thought and hurried to clear the remains left by the coven.

'Where've you been?'

'Oh, just reading the paper, sorry dear.'

Not surprised by the greeting, George headed across the soft carpet to the coffee table to retrieve the remains of the feast. He didn't look at the women for fear of provoking a new attack. He felt like an interloper, the lounge being a place that he rarely visited. Hildegard decided to demonstrate her control: 'I've decided that you'll need to decorate Arthur's old room. Since you drove MY SON away I can't stand to go in there where all his things are, it upsets me, it'll have to be changed as soon as possible. So instead of idling away your time reading the paper, you can do something useful.'

'Oh, very well dear,' George said quietly.

'Soon, I mean soon, don't think you can put it off, I need it doing quickly.' Hildegard turned to her friends with a look of triumph, a look which said, 'see my control, this is how to keep them in order.' The other two cuddled themselves in delight. What a great leader they had, how dominant over a mere man, this was how things should be done.

George said nothing, gathered the crockery together on to a tray and carried it out to the kitchen, receiving a parting shot to be careful with the bone china. As he placed the cups and plates by the sink ready for washing, he experienced a peculiar sensation: he felt reduced, smaller, as though his experience in the lounge had removed some of his substance. He still had all his limbs but he seemed somehow less of a man. 'It's happening', he muttered to himself, grimly, 'I'm being gradually emasculated.'

*

George's previous experience helped him to understand that his wife's tirade on the previous day had been to demonstrate her power in front of her friends, he also knew, however, that her attack had also been an instruction. He was sure that the room in question did not need redecoration because he had already done it when Hildegard had decided that the room required more subtle, pastel colours for her talented and artistic son. He might, in the past, have raised an objection but years of conditioning had broken his spirit, he had no option but to obey without question, completely unable to resist any of her demands. Early next morning, he set off to the DIY store down the motorway. It was, of course, out of the question that he should make any decisions, so he collected printed information about the materials that would be required to complete a redecoration of Arthur's old bedroom; colour charts, wallpaper pattern books, swatches of suitable fabric for curtains and carried them home for his wife's consideration.

He entered the kitchen and found his mistress sitting at the breakfast bar reading a magazine and enjoying scrambled eggs and bacon.

'I've brought these,' he said, nodding towards the armful of documents he was holding.

'Oh, well I'm busy as you can see,' she said without raising her eyes. 'Just put them on the table and I'll look later. You can get your stuff ready in the garage and I'll let you know which materials you'll need.'

Without speaking, he did as told and went out to the garage to find paint brushes, aluminium steps, paste buckets, pasting table and the other equipment that he kept for such an eventuality. The brushes were on the top shelf that ran the length of the wall. Reaching up he found, to his surprise that his arms didn't seem long enough and he had to use the steps. This was strange, he was sure that, in the past, he had been able to get items of that shelf while standing on the ground.

Having collected everything he required, George picked up yesterday's newspaper and sat down for a quiet moment.

'Don't you be sitting down!' Hildegard burst into his sanctuary. 'You'll need to get these things from the shop straight away if you're to make progress today. Don't forget, I want this job out of the way, that room is upsetting me, I need it changed.'

She presented George with a list of wallpaper, paint and curtain material along with a fifty pound note. 'I'll need the receipt for my accounts,' she barked, looking round and sniffing. 'This place stinks,' was her final comment before stalking out back to the kitchen and another cup of coffee.

An hour later, after a return visit to the DIY store, he began work scraping off the old paper which took the rest of the day. Next morning he rubbed-down the paint work and then moved the furniture to the centre of the room and packed books, trophies and posters into a packing crate before carrying it into the garage for storing until Arthur was able to take whatever he wanted to keep. Passing through the kitchen, he was informed that Hildegard would visit tomorrow evening to see his progress. He was about to point out that this was only the preparatory stage but decided against it and just nodded and walked on.

For several days, things went well. Apart from intermittent inspection visits that usually resulted in small complaints, he had painted the ceiling and the woodwork and was ready to begin papering. Occasionally standing back, George tried to see his work through his wife's eyes, since what *his* opinion was of no importance. He thought how strange it was that the room looked so much bigger without Arthur's furniture and belongings.

George enjoyed wallpapering best. There was something pleasurable about slapping paste on a large sheet of paper and then getting it on the wall and using the papering brush to create a smooth finish. He liked the way the pattern linked up and created an overall effect. Having finished one wall, he was almost looking forward to the inevitable inspection. He should have known better…

'I don't like it, it's the wrong colour and the pattern's awful! You'll have to change it. I can't live with it.'

George shrank inside. To him the wall looked fine. The colours were harmonious and the pattern well-suited for creating a restful atmosphere in a spare bedroom. He was about to voice an opinion when the rant continued; 'didn't you realise how dreadful it is? That's just typical of you, you just plough on regardless with no thought to appearance, couldn't you see that I wouldn't like it? Stand up straight will you.'

The tirade left George speechless. Why 'stand up straight'? He thought. I am standing up. Suddenly she wasn't there, having stormed out of the room, only to return minutes later with a sample of wallpaper torn from the book he had brought. 'Here this is better. Go get rolls of this one and do it again.' The final instruction was almost a scream.

The new paper rolls felt almost too heavy to carry from the store. The cashier said,'

42

shall I get someone to help you sir? George looked at him puzzled and embarrassed then simply shook his head. He managed to get his arms round the package, took it to his car and made his way home peering through the steering wheel. 'I'll have to adjust the height of this seat,' he thought.

After scraping off the 'unsuitable' one, he began to redecorate, finding the whole process very tiring. He wondered if his fatigue was a result of his advancing years or maybe the stress of the whole business was beginning to tell on his physical condition. One good thing, however, was that Hildegard had informed him that she simply hadn't time to carry out regular inspections and intended to allow him to complete the job and, at that point, she would approve or otherwise of his efforts. This was a mixed blessing because, as the work progressed, he became increasingly anxious about the final inspection, wondering if he might be required to start again from scratch. This thought filled him with dread; he was convinced that he simply would not be able to cope with such an outcome. Nevertheless, he was pleased to get on with the work without interruption. He was just a bit worried that his arms didn't seem long enough and he kept dropping the paste brush.

Hildegard had arranged for a meeting of the coven to coincide with the anticipated completion of George's work. The ladies arrived and were entertained as usual with fine crockery, a wide selection of pastries and Earl Grey tea. (They didn't really like Earl Grey but it sounded so much more refined than the other types with names that were too common or sounded foreign.) Gossip flowed well and local acquaintances were maligned in their absence. Finally, after a very pleasurable afternoon, the hostess announced that they were to see the results of her management of the redecoration. This was unexpected and created a very satisfying flutter of excitement. The hostess led her followers up the stairs and, without knocking, strutted into Arthur's erstwhile bedroom.

The floor was covered with piles of the unsatisfactory wallpaper, shredded as it had been stripped from the wall. There were also pools of paste so that strips of paper stuck to their shoes as they burst in. While the ceiling and woodwork had been painted, the walls bore the newly chosen wallpaper only in the lower portions, which started about halfway up near the window and gradually lessened as they progressed around the room until the final piece only covered about two centimetres at the base of the wall. By the side of this last piece lay a pile of clothes, covered with paint splashes and soaked in paste.

The ladies gazed at the shambles, awestruck, unable to speak, until Hildegard recovered from the shock and screamed, 'George where are you? You idiot, what have you done?'

The silence that followed was oppressive until a tiny voice, emanating from nowhere said, 'hope you like it, hope you like it, hope you li...''

Daisy stopped and looked around for any reaction. No-one spoke until I couldn't contain myself, 'what's happened, where's he gone?' Once again a flying cushion bounced off my head.

'Michael, remember the title, what's the story called?' Dad spoke. 'And Josh, stop throwing cushions.'

'Oh ... I see, you mean he's gone, like ... disappeared ... I get it, good one Daisy.'

'Thanks Michael.'

'How about that one Grandpa?' Mum asked, looking at the old man to make sure he wasn't asleep, despite having his eyes shut, but she needn't have worried.

'Wonderful,' he said, wiping his eyes, 'as good as the last one. Thanks Daisy, you're brilliant.'

Somebody clapped and then we all joined in.

'Oh, stop it,' said Daisy, 'it's just a silly story.'

It was a fine week; mid-summer August days stretched before us and Josh and me couldn't wait to get outside. Dad was working of course, as were Christine and Bob. Zachary was supposed to earn some money for the rental on his shared student flat but seemed to spend a lot of time lounging about waiting for Hermione. Josh was usually down at the local park supposedly playing tennis but he and his friends, including a number of girls, spent most of the time laughing and talking on the park benches. As for me, I had a good friend called Ian and we loved to be out in the fields that were only a few minutes walk from our house. We had befriended a local farmer who, unlike most of his kind, liked youngsters around and gave us little jobs to do, such as getting the cows in for milking, feeding the hens and doing simple repair jobs.

Despite our various activities, on the appointed day (every Friday), as 'story time' approached, we all managed to make our way to the big sitting room in good time to meet our narrator. Today, Daisy was first there, typing on her computer.

'Just sorting a bit out,' she said, without looking up.

After about ten minutes she struck a key with an air of finality, raised her head and smiled at us.

'This one is only just ready, I haven't thought of a title yet. Maybe someone could suggest one when you've heard it.' She looked at John Willy, 'this is a bit different Grandpa, I hope it's alright.'

The old man just smiled reassuringly, 'I'm sure it will be great, love.'

With this thought Daisy began in her calm, quiet voice: 'It's about a man called Herbert …

Herbert often lay awake when he first went to bed; he liked to listen to his wife's quiet, regular breathing and hear the wind soughing through the branches of the old ash tree in the garden. It was a time to gather-up the day, to think through the conversations he'd had with colleagues, to consider the meanings behind their words and actions and to rehearse what he should have said to them and would definitely say if the same situations ever happened again. He knew this was unlikely but couldn't stop himself from going over the old ground. If anything particularly puzzling had happened, he could lie awake for hours on a spinning wheel of worries. Equally, if he'd had a pleasant day, he enjoyed repeatedly running over the positive interactions, sinking gradually into a warm, dark soup of sleep.

This night something was different: a noise. When he first heard it, he thought that a wagon was grinding up the trunk road that climbed the steep hill towards the city. Despite the intervening trees and fields, they could often hear the traffic when the wind was in the right direction. It was a strange sound, like the rhythmic throbbing of a hard working engine. He waited, listening for the change of gear as the wagon reached the top of the rise; you could almost feel the relief of the tired gear boxes as they relaxed into a higher and less strenuous ratio, but it didn't happen, the steady beat continued unchanged. Must be the central heating, he thought and returned to his review of the day before falling into a restless slumber.

The next day was bright and cold. A glittery, uneasy sun had little warmth against the north wind. Herbert thought of the distant icy wastes that gave birth to the chilled air. He imagined the rustling of a forest of black trees on a mountainside, drifts of blank, white snow, the cry of a wolf as penetrating as the sound that disturbed his sleep. He shivered.

The eight-fifteen monorail carried him into town and delivered him to within five minutes walk of the towering block that housed his office. Herbert liked the city in the mornings; everyone purposeful, businesslike, an exciting mixture of people. He enjoyed the sounds of traffic, talk and movement that surrounded him; it was his town, he had a place in it, somewhere to go, a path to follow, a reason for his life. Yet, that day he felt uneasy, although the weather was cold and there was freshness in the air but, even so, it was as though the atmosphere was tainted, a dispiriting torpor settled on him, a background of irritation coloured his day; a strange and persistent rhythm echoed in his head.

In the lift to his floor it was gone; the metal case seemed to protect him. The air was calm and still, his spirit lifted, 'just the city noises', he said to himself. He watched the floor numbers light in turn and felt the deceleration as his level approached. Punching his code into the key pad on the main door, he walked briskly into the reception area of his office, nodded 'good morning' to the security guard and pushed through the double doors into the room that contained his work station. 'Work station', he hated the phrase, Herbert had been much happier in his old office with a door, a desk and a filing cabinet all to himself. But now he had to share with other minions; it was one of the economies of scale that the managers were so fond of creating. Nevertheless, despite their best efforts to reform working practices, he had managed to maintain a small 'empire' by leaving some of his papers on a particular area of the large open desk, making it clear that this was the space where he worked. The other workers recognised his need and left the area untouched.

It was back. Before he reached his workspace the rhythm returned; an almost imperceptible vibration entered his head. Herbert decided to ignore the noise, if it was a noise, he couldn't really decide whether he was hearing it, feeling it or if it was somehow just inside him, and if it was inside, was it in his head or somewhere else in the depth of his body? 'Maybe I'm over tired', he thought. After all he had been working hard recently; lots of meetings, documents to produce, and waiting for the bosses to approve or disapprove of his efforts. Perhaps he needed a holiday, a break, a change of scene. But enough of day-dreaming, he had work to do, time to settle down. The computer monitor burst into life as he touched the mouse. He called up his project file and began typing; the report was overdue and must be finished today.

More workers arrived, some spoke, others just nodded, most ignored Herbert altogether. The life of the office picked-up; chattering keyboards, hushed conversations, the telephone birds began their morning chorus and printers spewed out piles of A4. For a while he was immersed in his task; it was as though his mind had been preparing during the night and words flowed from him onto the screen. Herbert was pleased; he felt that his succinct analysis of the cost implications of creating the new product would be useful and well-received on the fifteenth floor, where all the decisions were made and up to which he rarely ventured. He almost forgot the noise but it was still there and gradually began to intrude on his consciousness. He tried to ignore it but it seemed to creep on to the screen; the lines of type began to waver, the hum of the server started to echo the beat, it was as though he was becoming cocooned in a shell of vibration.

*

'Tinnitus', the doctor's instant response to Herbert's description of his problem, 'Ignore it and it will probably disappear, try to think of something else, forget about it'. If it persists, we'll try syringing.'

But the doctor was wrong, even after syringing, it didn't disappear, instead it became more significant, taking on the steady rhythm of time itself, there was something ancient and immutable about its quality. It was here to stay, whether he liked it or not, the sound was now part of his life and he would have to learn to live with it. His wife, Muriel, couldn't hear anything and became irritated by Herbert's depressed state; instead of talking to her about his day or listening to her stories from the bridge club, he just sat, rocking slightly as if reciting some quiet prayer. He went to the garage and fetched a woolly hat that was used when he played golf. He thought that pulling it down over his ears might block the incessant vibration, but it had the opposite effect and acted like an echo chamber. His head became a seaside cave into which the tide rolled back and forth, with an unending, consistent beat. Muriel sat watching him; her hair in tight, ordered curls and her plump body tightly corseted. She shook her head in irritation and went to bed.

There was only one place where he could escape: the lift in his office block provided sanctuary. Here there was no noise, as the doors closed, the sound was squeezed out, he could almost visualise it struggling to get through the gap but failing, relief flowed through his body as the aluminium doors clunked together. Here was the answer; whenever the rhythm became unbearable, Herbert went up or down for as long as he dared. Fortunately, apart from the occasional meeting, he worked on his own, as long as his work was emailed to the fifteenth floor on time, no-one questioned if he was away from his desk.

At first everything went to plan; if he felt the need, Herbert went to his refuge, and when rested, was able to return to his work. But people began to be aware of the regularity with which they found him in the lift; they also noticed how he screwed up his eyes until the doors closed. He became conscious of the questioning looks in his direction and realised that this could not go on; another strategy had to be found. Fortunately, there were two lifts and the solution was simple – one of them had to be broken. Arriving very early one morning, Herbert fixed 'out-of-order' signs to the doors on one of the lifts on all the floors, including the fifteenth, and blocked out the floor indicator lights with black masking tape. Now he had his private retreat; waiting for the right moment, when no-one was looking, he was able to enter and sit in his box until peace returned to his tortured head.

For a few days, the lift sanctuary worked well but he found it necessary to use it more and more often, to the extent that he was falling behind with his work. A curt email appeared on his screen: 'evltion of flex box file ovdue – reqd yesday' As usual, he grumbled to himself, no punctuation or 'pleases' or names of people, the use of stupid abbreviations – what on earth is an 'evltion'? Nevertheless, this was serious. He was only too well aware that things were not going well. Since the 2009 recession, business had dropped off alarmingly; no-one seemed to want the stationary goods that Offsup produced. Sales were well down and redundancies were already happening; two of the older administrators had gone and more would follow. Herbert knew that he was a small cog in a huge machine and his previous good work would carry no weight if it came to cutting wage costs.

In his heart he would have liked to walk away from Offsup. The work was boring and he hated the impersonal attitude that managers took when considering the lower orders. The recent email was an example; they couldn't even be bothered to address him by name or indicate who had sent it. On his few visits to the fifteenth floor he had been treated like a nonentity when he arrived, and dismissed with a wave of a hand when his presence was no longer required. In the entrance hall, a plaque on the wall suggested that the organisation was an 'Investor in People', but apart from the plaque there was little if any evidence of this investment in practise.

He dreamed about leaving and moving to something new and exciting, but what? He needed a wage. Muriel didn't work and there seemed little prospect of her dragging herself out of the bridge club to contribute to the family finances. They had no savings and their two sons were having enough difficulty providing for their own families to be able to offer any support, which he wouldn't have accepted anyway. So Herbert was 'it'; the bread winner, gardener, washer-up, driver and occasionally cook and cleaner. He couldn't just leave and bum around seeking new horizons. He was stuck. And now this email; he looked at it and it seemed to grow and come off the screen into his head, where it sat, vibrating along with the noise. Perhaps I could move my computer into the lift, he thought. Then I could do my work in there and not fall behind.

53

The move to the lift had to be done when no-one was around which called for more dawn trips to the office. He received unpleasant looks from cleaning staff. They regarded early mornings as their time. He was seen as an interloper; one of *them,* a suit, a day worker who couldn't possibly understand the dimly lit world of the cleaning operative and had no place in it. The shop steward considered calling a union meeting with management to complain that their work was being inhibited by a foreign body who acted furtively, unnerving the staff by his presence. Whenever they saw him, he was sitting at his desk, apparently doing nothing but watching them. This must surely be an infringement of their human rights. Several cleaning operatives had already discussed the possibility of suing for post traumatic stress disorder, having been surprised to find him sitting at his desk when they entered what should have been an empty office.

Luckily, before matters came to a head, the move was complete. When Herbert arrived at the start of the day, he simply waited till no-one was around and slipped into the apparently out-of-order lift. There he kept his computer, plugged into a fortunately placed power socket, and the desk and filing cabinet that constituted his required equipment. To demonstrate his presence he ate in the staff canteen, so that people saw him around, and then retreated to his private domain as quickly as possible, driven there by the increasing volume of the noise. The arrangement worked well: he received his projects through the wireless email, and in the peace of his sanctuary he was able to work with a clear head and absence of interruption. On the few occasions when he was summoned to the fifteenth floor he bore the noise stoically and managed to make sensible comments when required to speak. This was not often since the bosses only ever really listened to themselves.

While his work life improved, the remainder of his day became an increasing torment, until he discovered the Ipod. He was just walking into the reception area of the office, when a messenger boy arrived carrying a brown paper package for immediate delivery to the fifteenth floor. The receptionist asked the boy who had sent the package, but unable to hear, he had ignored her question and turned to leave. She called after him but he continued to walk towards the revolving doors and it was not until Herbert touched him on his sleeve that he stopped. He turned and spoke, pulling out the left earpiece: 'what's up mate?' He said.

'Er, she wants you,' Herbert replied, pointing towards the reception desk. 'What's that in your ear?' The youth didn't understand, believing that everyone would know about the earpiece. He simply held the object out dangling on the wire and allowed its inspection.

Herbert touched the object but didn't understand its purpose. 'Sorry son, I didn't mean to be rude,' he said, thinking that it was a hearing aid. The young man shrugged and turned back to the desk to talk with the receptionist. But, curiously, after talking he returned the object to his ear and walked out, so it clearly wasn't to aid his hearing. Herbert went into the lift that was operating and rose to his destination, wondering.

Later, as he headed home, Herbert paused to look in the window of a shop selling electronic gadgets and saw an Ipod with its attendant miniature head phones. 'I wonder how they work?' He thought. The thick, glass doors of the shop swung open, operated by a movement sensor, and he walked nervously through them. Inside, a spotty, tall young man dressed in a cheap suit and suede shoes explained the Ipod's operation and a purchase was duly made. Back home, after loading in his favourite operatic CDs, Herbert found, that while the noise was still audible, it was definitely muted by the glories of *Turandot* and *La Boheme*.

A problem remained: during the evening meals, Muriel wished to have conversations. Since she spent most of her time in the house, Herbert was expected to tell her about his day and listen to any gossip that she had gleaned from her coffee mornings with Irene from next door. Conversations required the removal of the miniature head phones. He felt that he could easily keep up his end of the discussions with a brief description of his day followed by the occasional strategic grunt to indicate that he was following Muriel's news, whilst still keeping in his ear pieces. This was not acceptable to his wife, however, so he had to suffer the noise during dinner discussions but as soon as they were finished he was able to retreat into the world of such masters as Puccini or Verdi. They often sat watching television in the evenings but Herbert heard nothing of the sound accompaniment since he was lost in the world of arias, duets, quartets and choruses.

In the mornings, he could now travel up to town and walk to the office in complete isolation from other human beings and with the effect of the noise considerably diminished. In his 'lift office' he was turned off the Ipod and worked silently at his computer. His life was now on an even keel. Consequently, his work improved: he could work quickly, and for some reason, the quality of his thinking seemed more perceptive than even before he became afflicted. This was noticed on the fifteenth and he began to receive the occasional email complementing his evaluations – this was most unusual and gave him a new sense of his worth in the company. Life was good – for a while.

*

'When are they going to repair the other damned lift?' Malcolm, head of section, gelled hair and pin stripe, aiming for the fifteenth floor, complained as they walked along the corridor to the canteen. 'It's been months now and nothing seems to be happening.'

Herbert, of course didn't realise at first that he was being addressed and remained silent.

'You've got that damned thing on haven't you?' The head of section leaned forward and rudely pulled the wire to dislodge the ear pieces, making Herbert start with surprise. 'I said; when are they going to get the other lift sorted? I had a party of Japanese here the other day and I had to fetch them up in relays. It was very embarrassing, not to say bad for the firm's image. I'm going to have a word with Taylor on the fifteenth; it's just not good enough.'

Herbert looked at the man but said nothing. He didn't feel that the head of section required an answer, just an audience. In any case, his mind was occupied by the thought of his subterfuge being revealed. If workers were called to mend a lift that wasn't in fact broken, he would be thrown out, ridiculed and certainly sacked.

After eating his cheese and pickle sandwiches, he returned to his sanctuary and spent the rest of the day worrying out a solution to his problem. Maybe he could find some way to damage the lift so that it could be repaired without suspicion. Or he could just move out and let them find the lift undamaged – no-one would be able to prove his involvement. Perhaps he could simply wear his Ipod around the office – why should anyone object? But he knew in his heart that these solutions were untenable. Wearing the ear phones while working would probably be frowned upon; to render the lift broken immediately after the repair, so that it could be his again, would have created an avalanche of questions and complaints to the building management section. The resulting investigation might reveal his guilt. There seemed no way out.

The next day, as a low winter sun sent a pale light through the higher windows of the office block, Herbert opened the door of the lift intending to remove his equipment. Most difficult was the desk; not because of the weight but its shape required some manoeuvring to get it through the sliding doors. He jammed open the doors with a wooden wedge, lifted the corner of the desk and dragged it towards the opening, grunting with the effort.

'Can I help you?' The voice, unmistakably female came from behind. Surprised, Herbert allowed the corner of the desk to crash down, narrowly missing his toes. He turned to find a young woman standing in the doorway of the lift. The image of efficiency, she wore short, neat, blond hair and a figure-hugging, dark blue business suit.

Flustered, he blurted, 'er, no thanks I can manage.' He thought that she must be one of the secretaries from the fifteenth. Scared of her because of her extremely business-like appearance, he determined to have nothing to do with her, hoping that she would get on her way and forget what she had seen. He turned back to resume his struggle, hoping that she would leave.

'It's alright; I know what you're doing. You've got to get out of the lift before the repairers get here, otherwise you'll be in trouble.' She smiled as she spoke. Herbert couldn't help noticing her perfect teeth but was immediately worried by what she said. 'Don't worry Herbert… it is Herbert isn't it? I know everything and you're not going to be in trouble. Let me help you, this is the reason I'm here.'

What else could he do? He wanted to ask her what she knew but there wasn't time. The sun was rising and people would begin arriving. So, together, they carried the desk back to its normal place and then fetched the other equipment. Despite looking as though she had stepped out of an edition of Vogue, the young woman was surprisingly strong and adept at moving heavy office equipment without any damage to her immaculate clothing and hairstyle, the high, slender heels on her shoes did not seem to inhibit her movement in the narrow confines of the lift space. As Herbert lifted out his computer, she turned and deftly opened the lift's control box. With long, pale blue finger nails, she extracted a small computer chip and bent it against the metal door, then replaced it. 'Now they'll be able to repair it,' she smiled again with a conspiratorial air. 'Right, that's done,' she said, smoothing her skirt. 'I've got to go now but I may speak to you later if there's a problem.'

'Er, can I just …,' Herbert stuttered, 'may I know your name?'

She paused, for once seeming uncertain, then she smiled, 'my name is Jane, I am here to help.'

'And just …' before he could complete his question, she interrupted

60

'No sorry,' she said briskly. 'I must go now… we may talk later.'

Smiling and putting in ear phones, she turned, clicked away on her high-heeled shoes and pushed the button to call the other lift.

Herbert watched uneasily as the indicator lights showed the lift rising to the fifteenth floor. He felt very confused: how could someone from the top floor offices know about his lift-bound activities? If she did know, then why hadn't she simply reprimanded him and demanded that he attend a punitive meeting with management? She had seemed so completely in control, making him feel like a naughty child caught with his hand in the sweetie jar. Yet she had not been severe, simply confident and understanding, even to the point of disabling the lift to make it appear broken.

The sound broke into his reverie, louder than ever. He reached for the Ipod leads and placed the phones in his ears, immediately recalling the moment when his recent visitor, as she departed, had done the same thing. 'Does she hear the sound?' He wondered.

The office began to fill-up. Screens glowed into life and the quiet chatter of keyboards started. No-one spoke to Herbert; no-one noticed his ear phones, so he settled to work, listening to La Bohême – one of his favourites. I'll just have to wait and see what happens, he thought. He had a strange feeling of optimism.

*

The optimism began to fade as time passed and nothing happened. Life continued much as normal, the only exception being a change in Muriel's behaviour. She became very solicitous of her husband; asking perceptive questions about his work and enquiring whether or not he had any special requests for supper. This was unusual; Herbert was baffled. Their life had slipped into a comfortable torpor. The couple hardly ever went out together and rarely showed any affection or concern for each-other. Held together by a marriage that was gradually losing love and passion, they existed like separate souls living in the same house. Why then was she suddenly interested in his day? For years she had shown only superficial interest in his work or in the people he worked with. His supper was usually presented on the table in a take-it-or-leave-it manner. Now he was offered a choice and even asked what he might like on the following day. Still, this was not something about which he could complain; indeed it made life a little better.

Also, contrary to his expectation, no-one seemed to mind that he wore the Ipod at work; they just left him alone as usual. He spent his days quite happily reading reports and statistics, typing out his evaluations and listening to, what he considered to be, the most beautiful sounds in the world. He was occasionally told to attend on the fifteenth, and while delivering the information required of him, he looked around for signs of the girl but he never saw her.

Days passed and, although his life was

generally uneventful – the way he liked it – Herbert couldn't get thoughts of Jane out of his head. He rarely approached anyone from the fifteenth unbidden but he felt a degree of frustration that his relationship with this attractive woman had come to such an abrupt end. He decided to try to find her.

After Malcolm, the team leader, his big boss from the fifteenth was Alistair. He was somewhat distant in his manner but had always been polite in his few dealings with Herbert. Knowing that Alistair arrived early every morning Herbert decided to try to catch him. The security guard on the entrance was surprised to see him walking in at 7am. He thought about demanding an explanation but, at the same moment, his bacon sandwich arrived from the local café so he decided to concentrate on this rather than intimidating the interloper.

Herbert didn't have to wait long. Alistair arrived and was a little surprised when Herbert nodded to him and pressed the button to call the lift. They rode together in silence until Herbert summoned enough courage to ask, 'do you know Jane on the fifteenth?'

'Who?'

'Jane, I met her the other day, she was very helpful.'

Alistair looked directly at Herbert as if seeing him for the first time. 'Are you sure you've got the correct name, you're telling me you've met Jane and she came from fifteenth?'

'Yes, Jane, she told me.'

'She TOLD you?'

Herbert began to feel uncomfortable;

Alistair's attitude seemed to suggest that he had done something wrong. He decided to try to extricate himself from what was becoming an embarrassing situation. 'Sorry, I may be mistaken, please don't worry about it.'

'No, er Mr... sorry what's your name again?'

'Herbert Squire.'

'No Herbert, I am worried, you'd better come with me.'

Herbert's heart sank. He watched as Alistair cancelled the highlighted number for his floor so that only the bright red fifteen remained seeming to glow brighter, like a threat as, they ascended. The journey proceeded in silence until the doors slid open and his boss motioned for him to follow. Feeling like a humble slave trundling behind his master, Herbert felt his body sag. The noise returned and, in the circumstances, he was unable to use his Ipod to drown it out.

He was marched down the aisle of the huge office to the end rooms which were known by the majority of workers in the building as 'the holy of holies'. This was the place where important government ministers and other significant guests were entertained. No-one from the fourteenth down had ever actually been invited to enter.

'What have I done?' Herbert worried, wishing he'd never opened his mouth.

Alistair knocked on the beautiful but forbidding door and waited. For what seemed an hour, nothing happened and then a doom laden voice spoke; 'enter.'

The noise in his head now increased to an almost unbearable level. Herbert saw little detail such was his anxiety but had the impression of soft carpeting and luxurious furnishings. Behind a huge desk sat a small man with huge horn-rimmed spectacles. His head was completely bald so that it reflected the overhead concealed lighting.

'What's up Alistair? Who's this?

'Sorry to disturb you Max but I thought you should meet Herbert. He tells me that he's met Jane.'

'You mean … our Jane?'

'Yes, Jane from the fifteenth.'

Max stood but didn't look much taller. For the first time he looked at Herbert. 'You've met Jane? When and where?

Herbert, now nearly beside himself, could hardly speak. 'A few days ago … she was on my floor … and she helped me. But please, I don't want to cause any trouble …'

Max came from behind the desk and took hold of Herbert's arm with a surprisingly strong grip. Herbert found himself propelled towards a tall cupboard like door in the wall of the office. With his other hand, Max reached over and opened the door. Inside was Jane, looking her immaculate self.

Herbert stepped back he was about to say something in recognition of the elusive woman but something about her made him pause. He looked carefully. She was not moving, her face, though beautiful, seemed to lack animation and her eyes, unfocussed, stared through him. Max reached and took hold of her hand, raising it up and then allowing it to fall, lifeless by her side.

'This Jane,' he said turning to face Herbert.

'I think … she's … not the same.'

Max looked at the figure in the cupboard and spoke, 'What is your name?'

Herbert took another step backwards as a metallic sounding robotic voice answered, 'my name is Jane.' The features of the woman remained still and her mouth didn't move as she spoke again, 'I am here to help.' The noise in Herbert's head stopped.'

For a few minutes no-one spoke, then Hermione asked, 'have you finished?' Daisy just smiled and nodded.

'But, er… who was the woman? Was it her in the cupboard?'

'I'm not sure,' said Daisy. 'You can decide. It's a kind of a mystery.'

'Oh, Daisy,' Mum joined in, 'you've left us with a puzzle, that's a bit cheeky.'

'Well,' Daisy replied, 'I think some stories should leave you wondering. Life isn't predictable and so if they are to reflect life, stories should be the same. You accepted that George had disappeared, now you'll have to decide who or what Jane might be.'

There followed a general hubbub as everyone voiced their opinion. Grandpa thought that a robot had been made to look like the real Jane but Dad suggested that maybe the robot had to be activated before it could operate convincingly. Daisy sat and smiled; enjoying how people were responding to her story, until eventually she joined in: 'so what about a title then?'

'Robot', said Joshua.

'Jane the Terrible,' was my offering.

'I think it started with Herbert hearing a strange sound, so call it that.' Hermione offered.

'Call it what?' Sometimes I can't keep my mouth shut.

'Sound, just call it 'Sound.''

Daisy smiled. 'They're all fine. It doesn't really matter let's use them all.'

The British weather confirmed its reputation for unreliability during the following week. High winds interspersed with heavy showers made everyone feel annoyed. The test match against Australia was cancelled, which ruined Grandpa's week, and those of us on holiday from school were driven indoors much to Mum's displeasure, so the normally peaceful house seemed crowded and full of people interrupting what everyone else wanted to do. We were not good at being indoors, particularly since it was supposed to be summer when we should have been enjoying outdoor activities.

Consequently, the week passed slowly and included several arguments. It was a fractious group that assembled to hear Daisy's next offering.

'Where's Grandpa?' Mum enquired, looking round.

'He's in the downstairs loo,' Dad

replied, 'Says there are too many arguments and he's decided to stay there, won't come out.'

'Oh, we're not having this,' Mum sounded cross. 'Josh, please go and tell that silly old man that Daisy's waiting and if he doesn't come quickly, he'll miss the story and I've no intention of taking his tea down there, he can go fish.'

Josh was about to moan about being selected to get out of his chair, when he realised that, in Mum's present mood it was best to obey instantly. I managed to grin at him as he left to indicate my awareness of his displeasure and received a black look in return.

Minutes passed and the tension grew. Everyone was quiet, waiting, wondering what would happen if John Willy refused to come. The silence seemed to increase until quick footsteps were heard followed by slower ones and there was an almost palpable sense of relief.

Josh bounced through the door and flung himself back into his chair. Next came Grandpa, looking sheepish.

'Sorry everyone, I just got a bit fed up with the weather and all the arguments and no test match. Sorry to keep you waiting Daisy love.'

Daisy, as usual knew how to calm the situation. She stood up walked over to the old man, gave him a kiss on his cheek and led him to his special chair. No words were needed.

'Today Grandpa, I'm taking you back to North Africa. Remember, you once told me that on your travels you went to a part of the desert in Jordan, where you rode on a camel, through a valley called Wadi Rum, then stayed a night in one of the long, low tents used by the Bedouin.'

John Willy nodded.

'Well this a desert story and it's called:

BIRD OF THE DESERT

The lowering desert sun spread a deep orange light across the scrubby dunes. Sayeed stood over the prisoner, the knife in his hand like molten steel. Kamal looked at the face of their captive who, a second ago, had been pleading for mercy. His next pleas froze in his throat and he could only muster a strangled croak. He was the one who had stolen from Sayeed but did he deserve to die? Kamal thought not but knew that this was not the time to interfere.

Sayeed's eyes were full of ghosts; they sent a shiver through Kamal's body, he had seen this look before. The man's chances of survival were slim. A chill breeze stirred the soft surface of the sand, picking up miniature dust devils and sending them scurrying into the distance. The captive was shaking but not from the cold, he could see the end of his life approaching fast. He suddenly found a reserve of defiance: 'OK, bastard, do what you will, Allah will carry me to paradise.' He bent his head to touch the ground and began a monotone chanting.

A desert hawk flew low between the dunes and shrieked a warning. Sayeed paused and watched the bird as it disappeared into the advancing gloom. Kamal knew he was disturbed. The rhythm of praying and the call of the bird had changed the atmosphere. Despite his cold, unfeeling exterior, Sayeed held the kernel of Islam in his heart. The call to Allah for protection and the screaming hawk seemed like a message, an omen; maybe he was being told that it wasn't time for this man to die. Kamal saw an opportunity. 'He's not worth the effort, leave the pig here – no water, no food, hours from the oasis – let him take his chances and then if he dies it was meant, if not, at least the fool will have learned not to play near our tents.'

Sayeed looked at his friend. Kamal was tall and slim, against Sayeed's stocky muscular frame. They were both burned black by the sun and had the narrowed eyes of desert dwellers, but where Sayeed had rugged, sand-blasted features with a hooked nose, Kamal was a classically handsome Arab with a high forehead, black lustrous eyes and a firm jaw line. They had been friends since childhood, their relationship formed in the dusty streets of Ul Takha, where they had learned to fight and to make the most of every opportunity for staying alive. Both orphaned in their early years, they got together a small band of boys who lived on the edge of town amongst the bones of abandoned houses that were gradually returning to the desert. The crumbling walls and sagging roofs provided some protection from the desert winds and the unremitting sun. For food, they scavenged, begged and stole enough to keep them alive. Sayeed was the fearless leader who sometimes acted impulsively, Kamal his lieutenant who tried to rein in his friend with words of caution, in an attempt to avoid their capture by the local police.

Now he was doing it again: giving Sayeed an excuse for not going too far. They smiled at one another, smiles of understanding born from years of living, working and playing together – complete empathy. He looked at their captive. 'You have Kamal to thank for your miserable skin,' he growled. 'Stay here and die or live which ever you like.' With this he kicked the thief to the ground, flung his cloak over his shoulder and turned towards the white camel, his prize possession.

Kamal followed, feeling relieved that the captive had been spared. Not that he had any particular love for the man but he knew what it was like to be hungry and desperate. There had been times in the past when both he and Sayeed could have died because they had been caught stealing; they might even have been killed because someone regarded them as a nuisance, a blight on the village. Now that they were relatively powerful, he thought they should remember the tough times and have some sympathy for those who were still struggling to exist.

'What got you fired up anyway?' He asked, 'what did the fool take?'

Sayeed turned and from the folds of his cloak took something wrapped in an old, roughly woven cloth. He carefully peeled back the layers to reveal a glittering object. It was cast in the shape of a bird – an owl. The wings, made of silver, were folded back and encrusted with tiny gems that imitated the pattern of feathers. The head set at a slight angle gave the bird a quizzical look, as though it was regarding their faces and wondering who they were. The bright eyes were made of lustrous diamonds. The back, breast and tail of the bird were exquisitely decorated with gems set in white gold. It stood confidently, balanced on spread feet which matched the silver of the wings. It was quite the most beautiful object that Kamal had seen. For a moment his breath was taken. 'It's beautiful,' he gasped. 'Where did you get it?'

'I cannot tell you my friend. It is better that you do not know. I can only tell you that many men search for this bird and I have it. It is as old as time and very precious. You must not speak of it to anyone. It has cost many lives and I do not wish mine to be the next one.' Sayeed looked hard into his friend's eyes. He knew that Kamal would not betray him but even the closest of allies can be tempted when great wealth arises. They both appreciated the value of the bird, the flawless diamond eyes alone were worth more money than they had ever seen.

Kamal was silent, puzzled. He could not imagine how his friend had acquired such a treasure and wanted to ponder the matter. He was aware that Sayeed would not tell him more but was intrigued. He felt an overwhelming desire to hold the bird. There was a stirring of some long lost memory: he knew something about this creature but couldn't bring it to mind.

Mounting their camels, the two set off across the sand towards the now crimson sun that was dropping rapidly towards the horizon.

The chill of the desert night advanced bringing with it the spirits that moved in darkness. They heard a distant call; a strangled cry, it sent a shiver up Kamal's spine. Maybe the thief was calling for help.

*

The oasis of Tulah was hidden at the base of a sheer cliff of ancient, red/brown rock. The descent to it was steep and even the sure-footed camels occasionally slid on the loose scree-slope. Sayeed's tent sat with its back against the cliff near the deep pool of water, formed by a sweet spring that flowed gently through a fissure in the rock face. The low tent was positioned so as to afford a clear view of anyone approaching down the slender track from the desert that most visitors would use; only the two friends knew of the side entrance that was hidden by the date palms. Inside, the floor was covered with richly coloured carpets from Kashmir and cushions were spread around to provide comfortable seating. While the men could easily have bought a house in town, they preferred living under canvas, staying true to their Bedouin roots. The lust to wander burned fiercely in their souls; staying in one place was unthinkable, they would have felt trapped. Kamal sometimes mused about jail, for they often travelled close to the boundaries of the law and might one day find themselves incarcerated, he believed that he could not survive such an ordeal and would prefer to die rather than spend months or even years locked away.

After a quickly prepared meal of goats' meat and dates, the two settled down for the night. They slept, wrapped in their cloaks, with knives and rifles at their sides. The dark folds of the tent moved slowly in a gentle desert breeze. Kamal was disturbed by a strange and troubling dream. A hawk flew screeching towards him but its wings were not made of bone and feathers, they were rigid with jewels and the bird had the head of an owl. In the background a dark figure watched as the avian hunter speared at Kamal's eyes. He awoke as his arm rose to protect his sight from the vicious beak. At this moment the veils of time fell away and he remembered where he had first seen Sayeed's bird.

As children they had watched with the rest of the village when important people passed by. On this day, in the heat of the afternoon, a caravan had travelled down the dusty main street, scattering the donkey carts and driving children from their playground, but this was not like the old days when camels, veiled palanquins and carts drawn by immaculate Arab horses would have moved slowly along, now it was a line of black Mercedes saloons driven by dark suited men wearing sun glasses, while their twin brothers sat alongside, ever watchful for any suggestion of danger. The occupants of the rear seats were hidden by windows of darkened glass and, to the children, seemed mysterious and frightening. The adult villagers watched sullenly as though only reluctantly paying obeisance to the visitors.

It had been in the second car where the window had slid downwards for a few seconds, perhaps to allow a privileged child a glimpse of the world of ordinary people. Kamal and Sayeed could not see the face hidden in the shadow, only a slender young hand holding a beautiful model of a bird so that it too could see the poor people outside. Then it was gone; the window rose silently and the caravan moved on through the village and off on the straight desert road to Akabar.

The boys didn't speak but just looked at one another. This was beyond their understanding; they struggled to feed themselves and stay alive each day, to ride in an immaculate black limousine and hold a delicate, beautiful object in your hand was incomprehensible. How could such a thing be? They wondered. What manner of people were these? Each one stored away the vision because it was too strange, too alien to understand. They could not cope with the idea of such an existence.

Now the bird was here. That it was the same one was beyond question, the image had been burned on Kamal's memory. Then the worrying questions fell into his mind: how had Sayeed acquired it? To whom did it belong? Who was the creep? Was he the rightful owner? It never occurred to him that Sayeed might actually own the bird; he could never have afforded such a gem. Kamal immediately felt in his heart that deep trouble could accompany this exquisite creature. A bleak and forbidding outcome was imminent. He knew it. Maybe this time Sayeed had gone too far beyond the limits of Kamal's ability to protect him.

Without intending to, Kamal had become an important figure in the community. His influence and reputation had grown beyond the boundaries of the village, even to the city called Ben Habir. It was a habit amongst the local tribes to have large families; children, particularly sons, brought blessings and, as they grew and prospered, helped spread the family's influence around the local area. But this man had no brothers and yet he was well known and respected. Despite the harshness of his early years, or maybe because of it, Kamal grew to be a caring man who exhibited great sympathy for the human condition. Providing you were honest in your dealings, he could be relied upon to provide help in your troubled times and joy in your successes. Word spread quickly through the families that here was a special man; hard on those who sought to exploit the weak, but a loyal friend to those who manifested care for the less fortunate. He was not above challenging the law makers but only where he saw rules based on inequality; providing for the rich and influential while penalising the poor. Both he and Sayeed were known for their generosity to those in need; many families had praised Allah for bringing these men into their lives.

Had Sayeed simply deprived a wealthy person of a treasure that would result in little more than an annoyance, but bring substantial benefit to their own group of friends and local folk, Kamal would have supported him. But this was different: this bird was a special thing and it belonged to a very powerful family, such people would wish to wreak vengeance on anyone who challenged their authority. The hawk had truly called a warning; a warning that could not be ignored.

*

      Troubled thoughts interrupted Kamal's sleep for the remainder of the night. He listened to the night sounds of the desert: scuffles followed by cries signalled the struggle for life and death in this unforgiving environment, tent posts creaked when the spirits of the desert pressed against the canvas and just as quickly they were gone on their endless travels, leaving silence behind. He was usually at peace in this place but the bird kept flying through his mind and it filled him with foreboding. He was at least clear in his purpose, no matter what Sayeed felt, the jewelled creature must not be found in their possession. Whether it was returned to its owners or hidden in some secret place, it was too dangerous to keep. The two young men were strong and had some status in the community but would not be able to resist the retribution that would arrive if their sin was discovered. It never occurred to Kamal that this was Sayeed's problem alone; his friend might have committed a rash deed but there was no time for recrimination, it was now a shared situation that needed a joint solution. He knew why Sayeed had lusted after the bird. When you are born with nothing and have to fight just to stay alive, something as beautiful as that figure can seem irresistibly attractive. This bird would seem an absolute luxury that would excite every acquisitive strand of his being. Given the opportunity to possess such a thing, Sayeed would have found it impossible to resist.

*

In the grey dawn a soft movement brought them both instantly awake; years of living with danger had taught them to remain alert even in their slumbers. There was a soft bump and something rolled across the carpets towards their beds. 'Here is your friend,' a harsh voice filled the tent. 'He told us your names immediately but we could not let him live.'

The head had distorted features, stained with blood but was still recognisable as the creep. It came to rest at Sayeed's feet. One eye open seemed to observe him sadly. Sayeed was already on his feet, crouched with knife in hand, ready to fight. Kamal's hand moved towards his rifle and then returned to his side as five men, all carrying Kalashnikovs, pushed through the canvas opening and stood with their weapons covering the two friends. Resistance was clearly useless, they were outnumbered and outgunned.

The one who had spoken came behind, followed by a slight figure dressed in a black niqab with only the slit through which midnight eyes surveyed the scene. A woman! Why was this? A woman in the night desert in the company of hard men capable of taking someone's head; Kamal was astounded. She stepped to one side seeking the shadow of the tent. The voice spoke again. 'You will know why we are here. You have something that belongs to us. So that there is no misunderstanding, I am talking about the owl of Ul Haq. It is very valuable and must be returned immediately, or you will join your friend.' he said indicating the bleeding mess with the toe of his boot. 'Bind them,' he continued, 'we must teach them that we are in earnest.'

Having searched the tent and the area around, the men turned their attention to the two prisoners; the beating that followed was professional and efficient. Kamal knew that Sayeed would die before giving any information and indeed he hardly uttered a sound despite the pain that he must have felt. Both men were well aware that death would follow the return of the bird; such men as these would not wish it to be known that someone had stolen from them and lived. They had little hope of survival for the beating itself could have only one outcome. They prepared their minds for the end.

It was the woman who spoke as she stepped from the shadows. Her soft, soothing tones seemed incongruous in this night of violence and fear. Despite the gentleness of her tone it carried authority. Everyone listened, even the desert wind paused. 'Stop, it is no use, you can see their strength. They will die rather than tell what they know. We must find another way.'

'There is no other way,' snarled the leader.

'But what is the good of their deaths if the bird is not returned? It could be that they know nothing. Let me try to speak with this one, we know him.' She stepped through the men and stood fearless in front of Kamal.

'You are Kamal are you not?' He could hardly speak through his swollen lips so lowered his head to acquiesce. 'And you are known as a man of honour.' To this he did not respond. 'Do you men have the bird?' Kamal slowly shook his head. The woman's black eyes sought his. He felt her gaze penetrate his soul. She turned and looked at the leader. 'I believe him.' The man snorted his contempt for this idea but did not resist.

She turned again to Kamal and spoke so softly that the others would not have heard her words. 'This bird belonged to my ancestors. It has come through time through each generation of our family. It is important to me not because of its value but because it was held by all the women in my family who have gone before. You must know that whoever has it will gain no pleasure or profit; it cannot be sold and we will eventually find the thief and I will not be able to prevent his death.' She paused and seemed to weigh her next words carefully. Leaning close to Kamal, she whispered in his ear: 'I visit the market in Ben Habir on the last day of every month, bring the bird or information of its whereabouts to me there but tell no one. If Nazeem hears of this, you will surely die.'

Kamal's pain left his body he felt the sweetness of her breath on his face, her perfume filled his senses. His mind reeled as his very being was invaded by images of dark, lustrous hair, soft, firm skin, warm delicate lips and an exquisite touch. He was overwhelmed by her presence.

'Will you help me?'

Her words were simple yet she had immense inner strength. He was totally unable to resist. Through his bleeding, swollen lips he breathed agreement. She stepped back and immediately he was cold and in pain; he longed for her nearness to return but she turned away. 'Come away now.' She spoke the command quietly but in the manner of one who expected to be obeyed. No one spoke. Two of the attackers freed the friends from their bonds and then left. The complaints of camels roused from their rest signalled their departure.

*

Both men had bruised ribs from the severity of the beating. Anwar, who brought supplies out to the tent, discovered them the next day. He went to fetch help. Sadika came and helped bind their wounds then made soup from goat's meat, and bread from their store of flour. It was several days before, although still bruised, they began to feel able to move.

Eventually, Sayeed questioned Kamal

about the bird. He had been amazed when the attackers had been unable to find it. 'I know you cannot lie,' he said. 'You told the woman that we did not have it so where is it? Who has it now? Have *you* now stolen it from me?'

Kamal smiled through his pain. 'Do you think I would steal from you? Are we not friends?'

Sayeed immediately relented: 'I am sorry; I should not say this to you. But where is the bird?'

'Come I will show you.' Kamal took his friend outside and pointed up the sheer rock face behind their tent. 'It is up there, I gave it to the hawk.' With this he started climbing, gripping the rock with his sore and damaged fingers. Ignoring the pain in his chest, Kamal pulled himself upwards until he reached the tiny rock ledge on which the hawk had her nest. Sitting there was a bald headed chick, just beginning to grow feathers on its wings. Beside it the figure of the owl glistened innocently in the morning sun. At this moment the hawk returned to her nest but instead of attacking, she rested, her eyes meeting Kamal's. He reached forward carefully so as not to touch the chick and took the owl. 'Thank you my friend,' he whispered. 'You warned us of danger and have kept us alive but now I must reclaim my gift.' The hawk relaxed, ruffled her feathers and raised a clawed foot to scratch her head. Who can explain how men and animals can learn to trust but she knew that her chick was not in danger from this human.

With pain still tearing through his body,

Kamal descended and handed the precious artefact to Sayeed but he refused to take it. 'No my friend, once again you have saved me from a terrible mistake. I stole the bird in a moment of madness. I wanted to own such a beautiful thing but you knew that it could only bring death. I am a fool.'

Kamal clasped his friend's arm. 'You are no fool; you are the bravest man I know. We are brothers, taking care of one another but you are right about the bird: it must be returned. Only the woman can be the owner, it is her right drawn from ancient times. You saw how powerful she is. She is also merciful but those around her are capable of anything, we cannot take a chance.'

'What is she to you, this woman?' Sayeed knew that something strange had happened in the tent. On the point of death, they had been spared because of something that this mysterious and fascinating woman had said to Kamal.

'I am not sure my friend. I am nothing to her but she looked into my soul and saw the truth. I only know that this is a special woman; she seemed to be inside me and yet we never touched. As when I looked into the eyes of the hawk, the wisdom of centuries was there. They seem to be one; the owl, the hawk and the woman, linked by something as old as time.'

Sayeed listened intently. 'Then you must take the owl to her, until we are free of it we are in danger, meddling in something we do not understand.'

*

Kamal kept the appointment. He wandered through the dusty avenues in the market at Ben Habir. Many there knew him and tried to entice him to their stalls with offers of special deals for an honoured friend. They wanted him to stay, drink tea and talk a while but he had one thing to do before he could think of accepting their hospitality.

There were many women wearing the veil but he knew her instantly. She walked as though she was alone, apart, even though surrounded by the throng of people. He approached, her eyes met his and her power once again entered his being. Helpless to resist, he stepped towards her and placed the small bundle of cloth into her hand. For an instant, their hands touched. He felt that the essence of his soul had been laid bare, he gasped ... then she was gone.'

I knew that Daisy had finished but I remained wrapped in the story. 'Was she very beautiful?' I blurted the question.

'You have to decide for yourself.' Daisy smiled as she spoke, enjoying the fact that I was taken by her words.

'He's in love.' Josh spoke, laughing.

'Shurrup,' was the only response I could muster. There were times when I found her stories quite compelling and I resented Joshua's intrusion.

Before he could respond, Mum spoke: 'It was a fascinating story Daisy, we all really enjoyed it, thank you. Now then you two, no more disagreements, I agree with Grandpa, too many arguments lately. I know the weather's been poor and kept you in but we're a family and have to be tolerant with each other. You mustn't spoil this moment, go and set the table.'

Quelled, Joshua and I did as we were told without argument.

As the next week progressed, the weather improved. I had a friend called Robin who was a keen fisherman. He had enough tackle to loan some to me and also belonged to a local club that gave him the right to fish a section of a trout stream up in the Dales. We had to use the train to Skipton and then walk a couple of miles but when the weather was good, it was a great way to pass some of our holiday time.

The forecast for the whole week was good, so we decided to drag our old bell tent out of the loft and get permission to camp for a few days in a nearby field. It was owned by a farmer who charged seven pounds a day with eggs for breakfast and ham sandwiches for lunch thrown in. We begged cans of beans, tuna and soup from Mum and packed them in rucksacks to provide acceptable evening meals. Anything else we might need could be bought from shops in the nearby town.

Robin is an expert fisherman. He casts the fly lure just over the spot where he has seen a fish rise to collect an insect from the surface of the stream. I seem to be completely hopeless, totally unable to find the correct rhythm for an accurate cast and, consequently, manage to tangle the line or get the hook caught in my clothing. Nevertheless, I love the landscape. My eyes are entranced by the high limestone peaks dropping gently down through scree slopes to meet the wooded areas and green pastures dotted with sheep. Despite my feeble attempts to become an angler, wading into the glistening, bubbling trout streams to find the secretive, beautifully marked fish is an aesthetic delight. I sometimes prefer to sit on the bank with a bottle of ginger beer watching the flowing casts of an artist in the beautiful surroundings, trying to freeze the moment and store it in my memory.

I can help with boiling potatoes over a camp fire for some butter-filled mash which, along with a sizable trout cooked slowly in his tiny portable oven for wood chip charring, makes a great meal for the conclusion of a lovely day.

As usual we don't sleep well on the first night. Our own excitement at being somewhere so different from our usual bedrooms, inconsequential chatter and the sounds of the country night keep us awake. We have no sooner fallen into eventual light slumber than the rising sun and the morning chorus bring us back to life with the promise of another Dales day.

Three days we spent there, then the weather threatened to change and the call of springy mattresses and soft pillows took us to the station and the first train home. Arriving just before lunch, we had to relate our experiences to the family. Josh wished he'd been with us and Mum was pleased with her present of couple of trout.

Grandpa listened and then told us about one of his visits to the Dales to do some caving. He said he and his friend had tried to find where the stream that flowed through Uther's cave eventually emerged but without success. Daisy immediately asked who Uther was.

'The locals say it's an old Viking name,' was all he could suggest.

'Did Vikings live in the Dales,' she asked, intrigued.

'I'm sure they did. I know a little bit about them. They invaded Britain from about seven or eight hundred AD and many settled here. I know they were fierce fighters and conquered York which they called Yorvic. They were great sailors with beautiful shaped boats. They probably came up the Humber. There was one called Eric Axeblood – gives you some idea about their fearsome nature.'

'Where were they from?' Josh wondered.

'They were Scandinavian, from Denmark, Norway and I think Sweden as well.' Grandpa continued. 'We had Saxon kings until they arrived but they conquered large parts of the Country and England was split, between Saxon and Viking rulers. In fact the Vikings travelled all over Europe and became feared in many countries. The French king gave part of his country to 'men from the north' which they called Normandy and in the end, I can't remember it all but I think William the Conqueror was originally of Viking stock and he became king after the battle of Hastings.'

'I've heard of that,' Josh again, 'we did that at school, King Harold got an arrow in the eye.'

'You're right Josh, he did and the Normans won the battle so William became king. Folk think the Normans were French but lots of them were from the north countries. You see Daisy, the Vikings had a big influence on our history and lots of British people will have Viking blood in their veins.'

I could see the light in Daisy's eyes, her imagination was flowing.

'I'm going on-line to find out more,' she said, 'see you all later.'

With that she walked out and we didn't see much of her until Saturday evening when we all gathered as usual. I'd mentioned these events to Robin who asked if he could come listen to her story. I didn't think Daisy would mind so I agreed.

She was already in her chair when we arrived and she just smiled at Robin, so that was alright.

'Grandpa gave me an idea when we talked about the Dales and the Vikings,' she said, 'hope you like it it's called:

89

UTHER

The battle raged. Three days of bloody conflict and, even in Uther's fearless soul, the expectation of their eventual defeat began to materialise. Despite their superior weapons and skills in close combat, the sheer number of the enemy and the lack of space in which to manoeuvre were beginning to tell.

They had been foolish. A combination of bravery and an underestimation of their adversary's cunning had left them defending a position in a narrow valley which was open at one end but otherwise surrounded by sheer, slippery limestone cliffs. About thirty members of the enemy horde overlooking the valley from above were sufficient to render impossible any attempts to scale it the cliffs. A man cannot use his sword and spear when he needs his hands and feet for scrambling up an almost vertical rock face. Shields might deflect the rocks and spears being hurled down but, under these circumstances, a man cannot climb and defend himself at the same time. Also, in the meantime, those guarding the retreat at the bottom of the cliffs would be massacred.

Uther raged; he hated the enemy to the point where he wished them all to be exterminated but he was also furious with himself. These loyal men, some of whom he had known since they were boys had followed his orders without question. In many battles they had fought side-by-side spilling the blood of their opponents and sometimes their own. The rewards had been great, Saxon gold was beautiful, their ale was rich and strong, their women were easily tamed and the land they left behind was fertile. So why bring them to this place? This land of rock and mountains was good for nothing but it was land owned by someone else and, therefore, must be conquered. His own obsession with ownership had driven him on; if land existed, it must be his. This madness drove him, even into a place that the gods had forsaken. Drunk with the ale of conquest and acquisition, he had led his loyal band into a trap. Always regarded as the master tactician in battle, this time he had been outthought by a miserable Saxon.

Although driven by a lust for power and conquest, Uther was intelligent and knew that a soldier's thinking had to be clear even in the heat of battle. They were losing ground and there appeared to be no opportunity for retreat but his experience told him to seek a solution even though the situation seemed hopeless. Leaving the fighting to his warriors, he climbed on to a rock to get a better view of the land around. Behind and on either side was a wall of rock and before them an overwhelming body of Saxon fighters.

His eyes toured the surrounding valley. To the right, steep walls of limestone contained occasional fissures that could offer footholds for climbing but, while one man might scale the slope, only a few would escape before the rest were cut to ribbons. Looking left it was much the same with the exception of an area darkened by a narrow shadow. Relying on his warriors to protect him, Uther scrambled round to examine the shadow more closely.

A spear crashed into the rock, sending off sparks and just missing his head. Without looking back, he stepped into the shadow only to find that it was in fact a narrow fissure slightly above the level of the ground but just wide enough to allow for one man to pass through. Uther clambered up and squeezed his muscular frame into the darkness beyond, thinking that though it might not lead anywhere, he would at least be out of sight of the men who were trying to bring him down. He had no illusions about the fate that awaited him should he be caught by the Saxon horde: after humiliating and painful torture, his head would be severed and displayed on a wooden spike for his enemies to mock and ridicule. He didn't fear death or pain but he wanted to be a part of legend; to be remembered by ancestors who might sit around on dark winter nights and tell stories about the exploits and conquests of Uther the Brave. To be captured and slaughtered was too humiliating to be considered. The fissure might be a forlorn hope but it was a tiny possibility in a desperate situation.

Tripping and almost falling, Uther realised that he must wait for his eyes to become accustomed to the dark interior of what appeared to be a narrow cave. Slowly dim shapes became jumbles of rocks and the rippling sound from near his feet proved to be a stream running from the back of the cave but, rather than running out through the narrow opening, it disappeared down a black hole in the floor.

He peered down the hole but it offered no help. The stream simply vanished and not even a small man could pass through and no air movement suggested a way out. Nevertheless, Uther could feel a soft breeze against the back of his neck but there was no indication of its origin. Stumbling to the back of the cave, using his hands as much as his eyes he found nothing but a smooth, apparently impenetrable, rock face. Still he could feel cold air against the side of his face. Moving to the left, still using his hands, expecting to feel the side of the cave at any moment, Uther was surprised to feel the wall turn away and he found himself groping along a narrow passage, the breeze against his face, stronger now, his heart lifted, maybe there was a way out.

The ground level began to rise and he worried that the passage might get too narrow for a man to pass through as the floor rose to meet the ceiling. Bending lower, he pressed on, desperate to find some means of escape, even scrambling on his belly at times. There were many twists and turns, some so narrow that he feared he might become trapped, unable to move either back or forth but gradually, instead of narrowing, the passage started to widen, getting higher. Was he mistaken? There appeared to be a faint glow of light; another turn and there it was, blessed daylight. Still scrambling, but with renewed vigour, Uther made his way up to a grass covered hole.

Pulling himself through, he crawled on to a level plain covered with curiously shaped rocks and tufts of rough vegetation. The faint sounds of battle from behind made him turn but he could see nothing. Sliding on his stomach, to avoid detection, the old warrior made his way to, what turned out to be, the edge of a precipitous cliff above the valley. Screams, cries and the clash of metal got louder. Below he could see a sad sight, bodies, some with missing limbs and splattered with blood, littered the floor of the valley. Men from both sides lay dead or dying but it was clear that things were going badly; his men were being pressed further towards the back wall, facing what appeared to be inevitable defeat. The Vikings were particularly vulnerable to the small band of enemy fighters on top of the cliff above the valley's end as they hurled spears and rocks without danger to themselves, cheering at each successful strike. Uther was tempted to charge round and attack to close their hated mouths but he knew that such an attack would be foolish. It was better that he remain unseen before returning to enable a possible escape.

No time to be wasted. Keeping low, he scrambled and almost threw himself down the hole. With no regard for the knife-like rock edges the warrior squeezed through the narrow passageways until he was able to leap down into the cave and return to the narrow entrance. Now back in the battle, he sought out the noble head of Athlen, his trusted lieutenant. Struggling through the heaving mob Uther managed to get close and shout his instructions;

to move the men slowly towards the cave entrance using their often practised strategy called the cartwheel, which in battle was a way of moving fresh warriors from the rear to the front ranks.

Athlan used his stentorian voice. One word was sufficient for the men to understand what was required and almost imperceptibly they began, slowly but surely, to wheel, turning left to right so that the men from the front moved round the wheel towards the cave. Uther waited by the entrance, watching out for stray spears, and gave instructions for the first troops to line the cave so that those following would be guided by men whose eyes had become accustomed to the gloom. The men moved as quickly as possible, despite the combination of weariness and wounds of battle. In single file, they filtered through the narrow fissure.

It took time but very gradually the plan worked. Most of the warriors who could still move scrambled into the cave mouth until only a group of about twenty elite fighters remained to protect the rear of the retreat. Uther was at the front of this group alongside Athlan. They indicated that they would be the last to leave the fight and despite the protests ordered their comrades to make their escape until only two were left. Back to back the two friends fought like demons to delay the eventual final moments.

Athlan was cut. His right arm hung useless by his side. 'Go, he shouted pointing to the cave but Uther knew his job. Grabbing his friend's good arm, he virtually threw Athlan through the entrance and stood across it preventing the following Saxons from entering.

When his friend had disappeared, Uther wedged himself just inside the cave, so that anyone trying to enter would be hampered by the narrow gap and unable to wield either sword or spear. The men lining the cave walls gathered round to help their leader but he ordered them to leave, asking only that someone collect water from the stream and drench him to provide cool relief from the heat of battle and remove some of the Saxon and Viking blood on his body. Reluctant to leave, the men appeared to be on the point of rebellion but a glare from their leader persuaded them to obey.

Eventually, they were gone and the Viking stood alone. Still the Saxons came and one-by-one they fell until they were climbing over the corpses of their comrades to reach their enemy. Pain and fatigue racked the whole of his body; he was on the point of collapse in his mind he knew he would eventually fall. Images of his home and family drifted through his mind as he fought with automatic responses to the never ending stream of warriors. Blood filled his mouth, he was near to collapse…

*

'I'm whacked,' Sam flung off his heavy rucksack and collapsed on a patch of grass under the shelter of the escarpment that they were about to climb.

'OK, let's have a coffee break before we

climb.' Sarah opened her sack and produced her flask and a packet of digestives. Sam smiled, she was so well organised. He simply planned the routes for their treks and left all the details to her. She was happy to act the role of quartermaster making sure that food, maps and correct clothing and equipment were handily packed and accessible as required.

Now sitting beside him, she smiled and poured hot, black coffee into a plastic mug, handing him the pack of biscuits to open. 'It's lovely here,' she said, smiling and laying back against the limestone wall. 'What's it called again, this valley?'

'Uther's cave,' he answered. 'I think Uther was a Viking but why people call it a cave, I don't know. Maybe there used to be a cave here and the roof collapsed. Or perhaps there's an entrance that got filled in.'

'Do you know who he was or why he was here?'

'There's a story in a little handbook I picked up a long time ago from that old shop in Clapham. It says there is evidence of a battle here in ancient times but the details are sketchy. I've heard that the Danes have an old legend about a guy called Uther who did something heroic but I've never heard the full details of the story. There is a sink hole that we can look at on the plateau when we get up there and some folks think that it could lead to a cave but it's never been opened up... The truth is, we don't know the history but the name has persisted. It's just a great place to spend some time exploring and enjoying the scenery.' Sam

97

smiled as he finished speaking, knowing that Sarah would not be satisfied with this sketchy tale and would be searching the internet for more information as soon as they got home.

The peace of the place settled on them then and they sat enjoying the food and scenery. The air tasted fresh and a bright sun lit two lapwings as they performed an acrobatic display, almost as if they were simply enjoying the morning.

The climb up to the plateau took about half an hour and was quite strenuous but Sarah, because of her interest in Uther's story, wanted to get to the top so that they would have time to seek out the sink hole. At first they could see no sign of the fissure but, after some searching, they found a narrow entrance with a small sign that had been dragged out of the ground and lay flat next to it. The sign said, ' DANGER, DEEP HOLE', and must have been dragged out of the ground by a passing farm vehicle or perhaps the strong wind that often blew across this high, treeless plateau, had moved it over time.

They replaced the sign and parked their rucksacks by the edge of the hole. Sam pulled out their rope and fastened it securely round his middle while Sarah put on her helmet and light.

'Right,' he said when they were ready. 'It should be alright for you to go first, I understand that it slopes gradually down, not a sheer drop but be careful and take your time. I'll hold you firm, don't worry and if you're not sure, just give me a shout and I'll pull you back. But PLEASE take it steady.'

His final admonition was greeted with a

beautiful smile. 'Don't worry love, I'll be careful.'

Sam allowed Sarah to enter the hole and then pushed his own large frame through the opening so that he could see inside. He wedged himself securely and nodded to let her know that it was safe to go down.

The light from their lamps was sufficient to show that the drop was not too steep and should present no difficulties for experience cavers, still they went carefully, knowing that caves like this often had peculiar twists caused by the irregular pathway carved by the ancient stream as it made its way through the soluble rock. The water itself had long since disappeared but even so, a trickling sound could still be heard.

There were times during the next half-hour when both of them thought they might have to turn back. The gradual narrowing of the passageway made progress difficult and it seemed as though it might peter-out altogether. Gradually, however, the slope began to level off until they found themselves on a fairly flat cave floor with a channel indicating the passage of a stream but once again no water only a muffled trickling sound. 'I bet the stream still runs here during heavy rain,' Sam guessed. 'You can hear it somewhere close by.'

Sarah was examining the cave wall at the far end from their entry point. A pile of rubble indicated that there had recently been some kind of rock fall revealing an area that must have previously been concealed. 'I don't think we'll be able to go much further,' she called. 'There's been a rock fall, pretty recent by the look of it but it covers the old stream bed and any possible way out on this side.' Aware that the crumbling of surface rock can reveal hidden fossils, she turned her light upwards to examine the newly visible white/grey rock wall. She was familiar with the fossil shapes and patterns that were often found in limestone but these looked unusual. 'Sam, look at these, they're very strange.'

He scrambled over and the light from another lamp gave greater definition to the shapes. 'They're huge,' he said, 'almost like human bones, that's extraordinary.'

'Oh, Sam look!' Sarah's voice was filled with something like dread. 'Look at this one, it's the shape of a skull.' Sam turned to see, alarmed by the tone of her voice. It was true the eye sockets and jaw line were quite clearly visible.

'You're right, it looks human.'

But Sarah had moved on, her voice now full of excitement. 'And here, look, a spear.'

The shape of the spearhead actually jutted out so that both sides could be clearly seen. 'Let's pull it out.' She was already grabbing the shape and trying to release it for the rock.

'Sarah, stop, we shouldn't disturb it, we need to tell someone so that it can be investigated properly.' But his warning was too late. The rock of the wall proved to be quite soft and the spearhead, along with part of a shaft came away quite easily. Sarah stepped back, surprised by the ease with which the rock gave up its captive. This was fortunate because, as the spear came away, the surrounding rock began to split in several places. With no time to speak, Sam rushed over and pulled her out of the way. An area of rock was crumbling. They stepped to one side and watched in amazement not just at the rock fall but also at the bizarre shapes that were illuminated by their head lights. Forms like ribs, skulls, leg bones, spears, shields and swords crashed to the ground. Then they were engulfed in a cloud of dust, coughing and unable to see anything for several minutes.

As the dust began to clear, much to their surprise, a light appeared and a new, cool breeze began to carry the dust back into the cave. Slowly the pile of debris began to be revealed. It was, in truth, a graveyard. Skulls with loose-jawed demonic grins greeted Sam and Sarah as they gazed in awe at the extraordinary sight. 'Oh Sam, what have we done, they're dead people.'

'Long dead people,' he muttered putting his arm round her.

The breeze continued to clear the air and the couple became calmer. They realised that the light was coming from an entrance to the cave which must have been very close to where they had been sitting earlier. 'Well I guess we've found Uther's cave,' Sam said grimly. 'I still think we need to tell someone, this could be an important find.'

They were reluctant to examine the remains too closely it seemed somehow disrespectful, so they just stood looking, still amazed by what had happened. Then - a noise -

it seemed to be starting again but now behind them and not the same. Not just rock fall this time, a voice, a recognisably human voice, a loud cry of anger and frustration. Detaching itself from the far end of the cave wall came a figure, a huge emaciated man, wearing a helmet on his skull-like head, from which the eyes were missing. Using two hands he raised a huge, blood-stained sword above his head and staggered towards the couple. Acting on instinct, Sam tried to push Sarah behind him towards the newly revealed cave entrance but she was immovable, frozen by fear of this terrible apparition.

The Viking staggered, cried out again, fell to his knees, rose again and staggered on, still tried to get to these new attackers. Once more he fell and yet again tried to rise. Cries of pain and anguish issued from his hollow mouth. At last Uther's enormous strength failed, he fell among the corpses of the enemy and his body began to crumble into the Saxon bones until it was impossible to tell them apart. The shining sword faded quickly to a rusty relic and the blood became a brown stain. His proud helmet crumbled instantly to dust. The warrior's final battle was lost.'

After a period of quiet to make sure she'd finished, Dad spoke first: 'Whoa, Daisy, that's a good one, kinda scary. What do you think Grandpa?'

We looked at the old man and were not

surprised this time to see tears running down his wrinkly cheeks.

'How do you do it Daisy? He asked as he wiped his eyes with a big spotty handkerchief. 'Michael and Robin go fishing in the Dales, I talk about an old cave and you turn it into a super story. I don't know how you do it love, it's wonderful.'

'Oh shush Grandpa, it's just one of my silly old stories I'm glad you like it. Will it make you stop talking about dying now please?'

The old man looked glum. 'Let's not talk about that just now.'

Robin looked at me, puzzled. I shook my head at him so he said nothing.

As usual, Mum changed the mood. 'Right everyone, it's time to set the table and get the tea going. Please stay with us Robin, hope you like steak and kidney pie.'

'Great Mrs Armistead, thanks a lot.'

The following week there was big news on the tele about the European Space Agency trying to place a 'Lander' on Mars. Day by day we watched the news as the rocket approached the planet. They only showed computer generated videos but they were sufficiently realistic to give us an idea of what was happening. When the rocket went into orbit around Mars, everything seemed to be going well until the moment arrived for the descent to the planet's surface and then something went wrong: the vehicle's speed increased to reach above safe levels for a soft landing and despite the scientists' best efforts, it crashed and two-way communication was lost. The vehicle refused to respond to instructions and back-up systems failed so that it was, to all intents and purposes, dead.

There was much consternation in the scientific community particularly since the huge costs involved in sending the Lander through space would be wasted if they were unable to gain any data about the planet's surface. Several explanations were advanced: the retarding jets had failed; the parachute had opened too late, or the distance from the rocket to the surface had been miscalculated. Whatever the reason, repeated attempts failed to get any response even from the on board scientific instruments so the project was a failure.

'I've got an explanation,' Grandpa grumbled, 'it'll be the Russians they'll have sabotaged it.'

This was greeted with groans. It was one of his well-known themes; when anything went wrong, the Russians were to blame. When president Trump had been elected, the Russians had fiddled the vote; similarly when Leeds United lost or his racehorse didn't win or the price of petrol went up, it was the Russians' fault.

Zack spoke, he was at home for some reason that I didn't know and it turned out that he knew something about space travel, 'They're experimenting with lasers now. Some astro-physicists believe that these light/energy beams could be used to drive tiny objects through space. If it works it will be cheap to operate, no fuel, and very, very quick. It will be possible to send young, annoying brothers into space and out of sight. Michael, stop gazing at Hermione, it's embarrassing.'

I felt colour fill my cheeks as I quickly lowered my eyes. Hermione put her arm round me and said, 'it's alright Michael, take no notice of him, it's nice to have an admirer.' This was nice but too late, my confusion was beyond repair. I spent the rest of the evening plotting the downfall of my hated elder brother and considering how much I would have to save up until my meagre savings would become sufficient to pay for his girlfriend and me to escape to New Zealand, which I knew was as far away as we could go so as to be difficult to find.

Saturday and story-time arrived. I was annoyed to find Zachary still here but pleased that Hermione was joining us. It seemed that Robin had also decided that his invitation for last week could be used again, like a season ticket. Daisy came in, checked that Grandpa was there, smiled at Hermione and started her new story.

'All this space talk made me think,' she began, 'and Zack's ideas about lasers … well if that came true, then maybe something like this could happen, it's called …

CONTACT

'It's some form of electronic communication but like nothing I've ever seen!' Helen's voice was a mixture of excitement and surprise. Hardly daring to believe what she saw, she continued, 'it's a bit like binary but with strange attachments to each byte. I could imagine that these attachments contain more data but I can't access them. It looks very sophisticated and may be capable of carrying more information than our systems.'

The tiny nanocraft, propelled by powerful lasers, had been launched 240 months ago and were now within sight of, what appeared to be, a totally new solar system. One of the extraordinary discoveries revealed by the craft was the incompleteness of astrophysicists' previous conclusions about of the nature of space. Vast areas thought to contain little more than the curious substance called 'dark matter' had proved to be more complex. Astronomers had been aware of the existence of distant black holes but were staggered to discover what had now become known as 'light tubes'. These were invisible to both optic and electronic telescopes but were similar in effect to black holes; they attracted solid bodies and gaseous entities and, it seemed, nanocraft. Consequently, the sudden changes of course that unexpectedly affected the minuscule craft had been startling.

Questions had always been raised about what would happen to anything entering a black hole, where would it go? It had been considered that bodies might disintegrate or that there may be a parallel universe to which black holes might lead. Now it seemed that the light tubes could provide an answer, since it was possible that they may operate in a similar way to their more sizeable cousins.

As the tiny craft travelled through the tubes, little could be seen and many of the instruments monitoring their movement stopped registering any data but as they, apparently, left the tubes behind, the cameras fed back images of what appeared to be indications of a previously unknown area of space, it seemed to be similar in many respects to the known universe but whether it was part of this or something completely different, was too early to say and no-one had the temerity to offer an opinion. Although the tiny cameras were at the front edge of optical instrument development, the distances involved were so huge that, unless they passed within about three astronomical units of a body, they were only capable of recording an incomplete, blurred image, lacking in detail. Nevertheless, stars and vague clouds that might be galaxies could be identified. Further, not only did the tubes attract space nanocraft, since these continued to move, the lasers driving them must also be bent; previously thought to be impossible.

At first, the images received were blurred but acceptable, gradually; however, pictures became dull and vague until they were almost fogged out. Despite the inadequacy of the cameras, the computer terminals began receiving a clear, repetitive electronic signal.

Despite Helen's best efforts, however, she found it impossible to interpret the code into something recognisable. Since this was her particular area of expertise, the team was reliant on her skills and respected her knowledge.

'I've never seen anything like it,' she said, looking up for a moment from the screen.

'Try putting it through the interpreter,' Amos responded. 'It will try all its inbuilt variations and might come up with something.

'OK, but it will take several hours for it to work through all the options. Don't expect a quick answer.' With this, Helen sighed, opened the link to the interpreter and sat back, reluctant to admit defeat but recognising that the machine could apply a wider breadth of interpretation more rapidly than any human.

Both scientists now turned their attention to the monitors. The foggy scene seemed unchanged. Earlier, the nanocraft appeared to be approaching a dimly seen planetary body with dimensions similar to the larger planets in our solar system. Then the scene suddenly changed as though a defensive fog had been generated. Although the nanocraft were moving at about one fifth the speed of light, they seemed unable to escape the gloom.

'It's almost as though they've stopped.' Amos looked at Helen. 'Do you think we should check with Norma?'

Norma was in separate area of the Drone Control Centre, known to those in the know as DCC. The facility was relatively secret. The government body responsible for managing news dissemination thought it better to wait for a clear outcome before broadcasting any information about the drone project. The Russians, in particular, always saw any new scientific development as a veiled threat, so best to wait until the results could be demonstrably free of international subterfuge. Norma's responsibility was to measure the speed, direction and temperature of the nanocraft and alert the team to any variations that might indicate a problem or external influence.

Seconds later, they had no need to contact Norma because she burst excitedly through the door, 'they've stopped, absolutely still, no movement, nothing.' Her colleagues stared, unbelieving. 'Come and see for yourselves,' she said, sensing their doubts.

Pressing themselves into the space in front of her monitor, they saw 'speed zero, angle zero, orientation stable, temperature minus 195 degrees'. No doubt about it, the tiny craft had stopped. The mist seen through the cameras may not be as extensive as it first appeared.

'Maybe the lasers have failed,' thought Amos

'Unlikely, they followed the pathway into the tube, so why stop now? You can see from the monitor that they're still operating but clearly unable to drive forward. Seems to me that some outside force is preventing movement.' Norma nodded with satisfaction at her own idea.

Helen added a note of caution, 'this is completely new, we're in uncharted territory like the old explorers. Whatever we think, no matter how plausible it seems, it's still pure speculation.'

The team settled back, content to wait and watch for any new development. Eventually, watching a fogged out screen and monitors that never moved began to lose its interest and the team decided that one person could watch while the others got some much needed rest, they had all been on shift for about ten hours and were not to be relieved by Team B until two days had passed. Helen volunteered to take first watch and the others retired to their bunks for some food and sleep.

Four hours had passed when Helen woke Amos. He sat up scratching his beard.

'Anything?' He wondered.

'No movement. The electronic signals continued but nothing else, just fog. Maybe you'll have better luck.'

Amos muttered incoherently and stumbled off to the 'obs' room, leaving Helen to settle into her sleep pod.

This pattern was repeated through three days until eventually even the electronic communication stopped.

The B team decided to call in the others. Norma was asked to maintain watch while the others discussed the current situation.

'I'm sorry to have to say this, but we may have to consider abandoning this project unless something happens soon.' B Team leader Margaret spoke first. 'We've had no movement and no events of any kind for four days. I cannot justify keeping six top level physicists basically observing nothing. Either the nanocraft have stopped completely or we're simply receiving a residual signal and the nanocraft have failed. Our readings tell us that the lasers are still operating but apparently having no effect. We have no plausible explanation for this. We are taking no new readings and the data we have collected so far just informs us that the lasers will successfully propel the craft for long distances, even into these unexpected light tubes. Now these in themselves provide ample possibilities for further study so the project has revealed new information and we may have to focus on this and how we can map their positions so that future projects can avoid them since it seems that entering them has caused movement to stop. Any suggestions or comments?'

Helen looked round for any clues as to what the others might be thinking but all she saw were tired faces and blank expressions. 'It was Norma who suggested that the nanocraft might be held by some external force,' she said without knowing where this might lead.

Margaret was a good leader and always open to suggestions. 'It's an interesting notion,' she said, 'and there may be some mileage in it but we haven't observed any evidence of an outside influence since that electronic signal ended and you haven't come up with any useful interpretation of it; what is it doing if anything? Where is it from? Is it a message? The nanocraft continued to move when it first arrived and it hasn't affected any of the internal mechanisms. Has the interpreter come up with anything?'

111

'It's hasn't finished the run yet. It is taking a long time I know but there are millions of possibilities to be explored. At least it hasn't presented a 'no solution' output.'

'Yes, thanks Helen, I sense your frustration and we all value your expertise but money talks and our backers will want to see some outcome for what is, I'm sure you'll agree, considerable expenditure. Any other issues or ideas?'

'Well, if we are to be shut down or reduced, what sort of timescale is likely?' Amos, ever the pragmatist, wanted to know how soon he might be able to return to his first love: the study of samples of rocks and dust collected by the Mars probe.

Alison, the youngest member, slightly overawed by the reputations of her colleagues, yet developing confidence from the respectful way they referred to her work on gravitational forces, spoke quietly, 'will anyone be asked to look further at the light tubes?'

Margaret paused. 'Er, well let's take Alison first. Do I assume from your question that you would be interested in such a roll?'

'Well yes, but I'm not intending to try to get in first or anything like that,' she said looking a little confused.

'No, we all know that Alison, don't worry. I'll make a note of anyone interested in that area and we'll have to wait and see what the directors think. Now Amos, we all now how keen you are to return to your rocks,' people smiled, 'at this stage I have no precise time in mind but …'

'They're moving!' Norma's excited voice carried through from the observation room, surprising everyone. Without waiting for Margaret to end the meeting, they all piled through the door and scrambled to the monitors.

*

After three days monitoring the now relatively slow movement of the nanocraft, the team was able to conclude that their laser drivers were now inoperative and some external force was controlling both speed and direction. The thick fog had disappeared. Whether the craft had moved beyond it or the force controlling movement had also cleared it away, no-one could decide. Nevertheless, once tired eyes and brains were reinvigorated, the project had new energy with everyone excited by the prospect of completely new discoveries, possibly beyond anything previously experienced. It was almost self-evident that since the nanocraft were experiencing some form of external control, there was a possibility, however remote, that an alien intelligence might be behind this unexpected influence.

The craft were now moving, at this more sedate pace within a system of heavenly bodies very similar to that normally observed from Earth. Indications of star systems, galaxies, gaseous entities and one movement suggesting a distant comet held the fascinated gaze of the observers. Excitement was so intense that teams were reluctant to change shifts in case anything exciting happened when they were absent. The electronic signals had stopped, leaving Helen, in particular, very frustrated especially since the interpreter had come up with a strange one word conclusion: 'glagolitic'. 'What's that supposed to mean?' She had shouted at the terminal.

Over the next few days, order was restored. Margaret indicated that people should return to their normal sphere of study and teams must operate under the regular shift system so that areas like speed, direction, temperature, radiation and electronic influences could be systematically measured and recorded, and those responsible for observing the range of astronomical bodies picked up by the cameras could ensure that images were recorded on video and any spectrometry outcomes carefully noted. The search for sources of mineral deposits that might one day help replenish Earth's dwindling stocks was particularly important and, for the backers, appeared to be the main aim of the project. Although the nanocraft were now moving at lower speeds, they were still exceeding anything previously attained by jet planes, intercontinental ballistic missiles or rockets so it was important that regular observations should be made in order that nothing of note would be missed.

Underlying all these considerations, however, was one burning issue: who or what was now controlling the movement of the tiny craft? Scientists generally are trained to devise hypotheses to predict patterns and outcomes, and then test their validity. Under these circumstances, they felt impotent. Any number of hypotheses could be devised to explain why the nanocraft were behaving as they did but the team had no means of testing their accuracy. On one hand they were fascinated by this turn of events but on the other, frustrated by their inability to understand exactly what was happening. In the end they tried to settle down to making systematic observations, which was, in itself, a fascinating activity but the evidence of their own eyes constantly reminded them that they were no longer in control. Until some explanation emerged, there was a worrying undercurrent to the work; whatever they discovered might be fruitless in terms of future exploration because some external force was in charge so that, whatever the team wished to do may not be allowed. After having passed, unexpectedly through the light tube, they had no knowledge of the nanocrafts' actual position. They could see bodies similar to those in the known universe but had so far been unable to identify any of them.

As the movement of the tiny craft began to decrease even further, they appeared to be heading towards a single star with evidence of surrounding planetary activity. Excitement in the DCC was palpable; the opportunity to study what might be an alien solar system was something of a holy grail for astronomical physicists. The only frustration was their inability to control the crafts' speed and direction, which meant that, even if they were able to identify the existence of a planetary body, they would be unable to move closer or slow down to make detailed observations.

Nevertheless, this would still be a unique experience so, once again, the shift system was neglected and the observation area was constantly crowded. People ate packets of sandwiches standing up and occasionally drowsed despite their uncomfortable swivel chairs. Images received showed that the nanocraft were passing through, in space terms, an area with a considerable amount of 'rubble'. Although this rubble consisted of lumps of rock hundreds and even thousands of cubic kilometres big and thousands of miles apart, the bodies were still small in astronomical terms.

Margaret called out results from the spectrometer readings concerning the nearest body which was, fortunately, one of the biggest: 'There appears to be some evidence of a ferrous content.'

'Look at the edge, there's a kind of haze, which indicates some sort of

atmosphere,' Alison added.

'It's mostly nitrogen with some methane.' Amos looked up from his screen, his face alive with excitement. He was happy to have some concrete information to impart after days of relative inactivity.

'How many are there?' He asked.

'Difficult,' Alison paused, thinking, 'must be around eight or nine hundred.'

'Be good to spend a bit more time here, I'm getting some indication of a much larger body but it's too far off the get anything definite at the moment.'

You're out of luck Amos, I think we're

moving again.'

'I'll keep working on what I've got - see what the computers come up with.'

All too soon, the nanocraft moved on, leaving the cluster of small bodies behind. Nothing near enough to study now, just the vastness of space so the teams relaxed. Some sought food and drink, while others decided to retire to their bunks, with an admonition to their colleagues to wake them if anything happened.

In the days following, the nanocraft began to accelerate, now achieving extraordinary speeds, all efforts to re-establish control were fruitless, direction and speed seemed erratic but never in reverse. Several days passed, their speed exceeded anything previously achieved. While there was little to see beyond distant heavenly bodies, nevertheless, the observers felt that movement was not random, a feeling summarised by Margaret: 'I can't help but feel that we're being led up an interplanetary path,' she mused.

Alison agreed, her eyes shining, 'it's so exciting, I haven't slept for about 36 hours.'

Margaret frowned, 'please take care; we may need to be at our most alert before this journey's complete.'

'Oh, Margaret, I think you've been on duty more than anyone else,' Alison grinned.

'Yes, you're correct,' Margaret smiled in return, 'let's both take some time out, we'll give Amos a turn, he's been asleep for about five hours.'

Amos was roused and took his place in the 'obs' room. Helen wandered in and settled alongside Amos but they saw little during their shift. The teams returned to their normal pattern of rotation of observation watches and days stretched into weeks with little happening. The only noticeable change was a continued increase in speed until the nanocraft were approaching the speed of light.

'If they enter any form of atmosphere, they'll burn up,' Norma observed.

'You must be able to predict the future', Amos growled. 'Look ahead.'

Heads gathered to get a better view and the scientists started to talk excitedly as they realised that the craft were definitely approaching a much larger body.

'This could be the end,' Amos again. 'If that thing has any atmosphere they'll burn.'

'Well, don't just sit there waiting to see,' Margaret, as usual focused on the job, 'let's get some readings so that we'll at least be able to report some data about the place where our nanocraft perished.'

The team responded immediately, returning to the various instruments that recorded and interpreted the data being transmitted. Soon voices from around the observation area began calling out information.

'Atmosphere mainly hydrogen and helium, some evidence of hydrocarbons.'

'Ice covered surface – water, ammonia and methane.'

'Rocky body with considerable ice content.'

'Some methane in outer atmosphere.'

'Is that why it looks blue?'

'Yes.'

There is a huge dark spot but I can't distinguish its nature. Probably a weather phenomenon, huge wind speeds … around 2000 kph!'

'Temperature in the outer atmosphere around minus 218 centigrade.'

'Whoa, that's bloody cold.'

'There's a faint ring but it's a bit fragmented … not sure.'

'It's huge … mass of around seventeen earths …a giant.'

'Volume around fifty five earth size.'

Information continued to pour into the room, everyone pleased to have something useful and interesting to do after many days inactivity. Margaret, however, skilled at holding and interpreting masses of data to get a more complete vision, began to feel a little uneasy; it seemed to her that this data had a familiar ring. Without checking she couldn't be certain but she felt that the team was describing a planetary body quite similar to one she already knew. Not wishing to introduce a thought that might interrupt the work and enthusiasm of the team, she retired to her office to check a few details and think.

The key features that prompted her awareness of a certain similarity were the blue colour and the dark spot. It took only ten minutes for her to confirm her opinion that there was an uncanny similarity between the data being received and some that had been recorded before. She returned to the observation area, wondering what she ought to say but needn't have worried, some of her bright and experienced team members had already reached the same conclusion.

'Margaret, we think this is very similar to the data we have about Neptune.' Others nodded as Norma spoke.

'Even down to the dark spot,' Amos added.

Margaret nodded and smiled; she should have known that her colleagues would have quickly reached the same conclusion. 'Yes, there are strong similarities. Not only the colour, the atmosphere, the icy surface, its size and the fragmented ring remind us of Neptune. But we have to be careful here. Think of the journey that these nanocraft have had, is it likely that they have returned to the home system, or are we simply looking at a similar body in a distant system. We must be careful to avoid jumping to a conclusion that will infect our approach to what may be entirely new.'

'Yes, your right of course,' Amos smiled, recognising that the boss was a true scientist – no conclusions without irrefutable, empirical evidence. 'We need to continue careful observations. One thing in our favour is that they appear to have changed direction so it's unlikely that they will enter the atmosphere.'

A buzz of conversation followed. Minds alert now, full of speculation despite the leader's urging to avoid erroneous judgements. Nevertheless, the team settled back to their observations and began feeding back information.

'Speed decreasing, angle to planet forty five degrees. They're moving away.'

Views of the planet gradually disappeared and life returned to a more boring pattern, little to observe but distant bodies and speed and direction of the nanocraft. Whatever was controlling their motion caused their speed to increase but beyond this there was little to observe or measure. Quite quickly, excitement died down and the two teams went back to their normal pattern; recording data formally for later analysis, taking rest breaks in turn and feeding hungry appetites. But there was tension in the air, fed by awareness that the next observations would be critical in identifying whether or not they had been looking at Neptune or a previously unknown body with similar characteristics.

*

'The orders are to stay with it.' Margaret had called both teams together in the staff room. Although, for several weeks, the nanocraft had transmitted little detailed information about the nature of their surroundings, the scientists were still receiving basic information about speed, temperature and direction. Visually, only dim images of distant bodies were seen but the extraordinary speeds being achieved suggested that they might eventually make closer contact with an astronomical entity which could lead to more scientifically important information and reveal whether they had actually been observing Neptune or some other body with similar characteristics.

The days were not entirely wasted since, apart from the everyday data, the gravitational wave recorder had identified a faint signal indicating a distant catastrophic space event. Ivan, from the other team, being an expert in this field was asked to suggest an explanation. After some consideration and attempts to get some idea of scale, he suggested that a wave of such magnitude travelling through space/time could be generated by a collision between two black holes. Since it was unlikely that instruments on Earth would have detected this phenomenon, this was vital information in advancing human understanding and revealing that black holes could be more numerous than previously thought.

This development had been useful when Margaret was called to a meeting with the directors, to discuss whether or not the project should be abandoned. Her presentation of new information about the nature of the universe and considerations about the matter of national security persuaded the members to allow more time. The reference to security was a useful ploy since the politicians, who made up most of the members of the board of directors, had little understanding of the important scientific data being collected but were paranoid that some other Country might steal a march in developing weapons or security systems that could facilitate or militate against the use of intercontinental, ballistic missiles.

'But I have to say, we can't go on for ever and I know that you all have other important work that needs your attention. They have more or less indicated that it will be our decision if and when to close this project. So I suggest that we give it another week. What do you think?'

No-one spoke but a general nodding of heads and murmur of agreement showed broad acceptance of the idea. The truth was that most of the team members were becoming bored and wanted to move on to more interesting activities.

'Fine,' Margaret continued. 'So let's outline the current situation and then prepare to draw this to a close. Amos, you're good at synthesising the essence where are we?'

Amos paused for a moment, 'speed has been around that of light, temperature varying around minus 250 to 300 degrees. We've observed distant bodies but, apart from one, nothing close enough for analysis. The nanocraft have travelled in the region of 10.5 AUs since they left the blue planet. We have no understanding of the controlling force; it has instituted changes of direction but no significant changes to speed until yesterday when they began to slow down, which, if it follows the same pattern as previously, suggests that they might be approaching something but we have no other evidence of such an event.' He paused again and looked round for other contributions but no-one spoke.

'Thanks Amos, thorough as usual.' Margaret also looked around to offer anyone else the opportunity to speak but any offers were pre-empted by a shriek from the obs room. Alison had been asked to continue observing during the meeting so that nothing of importance would be missed.

'Something!' She called, 'I think it's big.'

Meeting abandoned, everyone rushed next door to gaze at the images of a large, green, planet-like body being transmitted by the drone cameras.

'Please, let's take readings.' Margaret again tried to calm the situation.

People responded to her instruction and soon voices began calling out information from the range of instruments:

'Atmosphere, helium and hydrogen.'
'Ices – water, ammonia and methane.'
'Temperature minus 225 degrees.'
'Several satellites – numerous.'
Volume about 60 Earth size.'
'Rock and ice body.'
'Layered cloud structure, water lower, methane upper. High winds 250 miles a second.'

A quiet voice calmed the chatter. 'It's Uranus.'

Everyone paused and looked at Margaret. She spoke again, 'You're describing Uranus, the next planet after Neptune in our solar system.'

Total silence now, team members stunned by the realisation that the nanocraft had, it seemed, returned to the home solar system through a 'light tube' that they believed led to a parallel universe.

This, in itself, was astonishing but even more surprising was that, as Margaret spoke, all the scientific instruments measuring the information transmitted from the nanocraft suddenly stopped as though they had been turned off.

'Incoming message,' Norma, operating the radio receiver called out, 'I'll put it on the speaker.'

A heavily accented voice came through. 'We have intercept and destroy your spy craft. Be it known to all members of NATO that we of the great Soviet Socialist Republic have control your space craft since they enter the solar system and we have demonstrate the ability of our glorious scientists to destroy these machines as we wish. Our leaders will be raising the issue of this violation of our security at the United Nations. This behaviour will not be tolerate."

Daisy stopped and looked around, wondering how this story had been received. As usual, for a while no-one spoke. It was as though we all needed a little time to reflect and digest what we had just heard; her stories were so different and unusual.

'Russians again,' muttered Dad, 'they seem to be into everything these days.'

'Remember it's just a story,' said Mum, 'only Daisy's imagination.'

'He's right though,' Grandpa joined in.

'They stick poison pellets into people, fix the American election, buy up our football clubs, they're always up to something.'

'Hey, enough politics, did you like the story,' Daisy wanted to know.

'Sure, it was another good one Daisy,' Mum answered. 'You see how it's got these two talking, they think it's real.'

Zachary joined in, laughing, 'I know you make the stories up Daisy but that word, er... galgotic, or something like that, is that your invention?'

Daisy smiled, 'you really were listening Zack, no, Glagolitic is real it's the name of the first Slavic alphabet, used to translate Greek into Slavic. It was the base of the Cyrillic alphabet used by the Soviets. I just think it's best to keep the facts in a story as accurate as possible.'

'Great stuff, Daisy, good research,' Zack replied admiringly.

I felt a bit jealous. It's not often that he accepts that anyone else in the family is clever but before I could dwell on this, Grandpa broke in, 'it's also true about those Russians - into everything - you can bet your boots that if something goes wrong, they're at the back of it.'

'He's off again,' Mum laughed. Let's get the tea started folks. Everyone murmured approval. It's nice to be a member of my family.

Back to school now for me, Josh and

Daisy so the next week passed quickly. We all moved to new year groups but still had the same friends, except for Daisy because she moved into the lower sixth and some of her friends had left to start work or moved on to various training schemes.

Despite having the same people around, school felt different I was facing GCSE exams at the end of the year and people kept telling me how important these were for my future. It all seemed to become more serious: bags of homework warnings of interim tests to measure our progress and warnings of damage to life chances if we failed.

Some subjects I study because they might be helpful in the future. I'm thinking about getting into graphic design so 'art and design' is a must and I enjoy it. I also have to do the 'basics'; maths and English. English is OK but maths is difficult and a bit boring. Other than these, I was free to choose so I opted for history, geography, music and PE. They're all interesting in parts but history requires a lot of learning and remembering facts and dates. Geography though, I enjoy; how other people live and the range of environments is fascinating. It's also useful that Grandpa John Willy has travelled so much so he wants to know which country we're studying because he usually has a story to tell that helps to make the place come alive.

We've started the term revising the impact of geology on climate. Mr Squires the teacher gave us homework to find out how the Andes affect South American countries. I asked

Grandpa for help and he told me about Lima which is close to the sea but has very little rainfall since the land rises quickly because of the mountains and most rain falls at higher levels. Lima does, however, get a lot of mists which provide sufficient water for the city.

'When I was there,' he told me, 'we noticed that the streets have no drains. They're not needed because of so little heavy rain.'

I noted this information and thanked him but, as usual, he had more information and was happy to find an interested listener. He told me about the beautiful ruins that he'd seen.

'I've heard of the Incas,' I told him.

'Yes they built Machu Picchu which is beautiful and probably the best known site,' he said, 'but there are others. Did you know that the Egyptians weren't the only ones who built pyramids? There were people called Mayan who were very sophisticated and artistic and they built huge Pyramid type erections. One is well known at Chichen Itza but there are others few people have heard of let alone seen. A few are hidden in the rain forest and when you find them, they just take your breath away.'

'Were they around at the same time as the Incas?'

I was startled by Daisy's voice. She had come in quietly to sit with us in Grandpa's room but he'd noticed.

'No love, the Mayans were the first and then Olmecs and Aztecs but they all learned from one another and had similar cultures. Did you know they used human sacrifice as part of their rituals?'

'Oh, that's barbaric.' Daisy was shocked

Grandpa smiled and then continued: 'Historians think that they were trying to please their gods, like the sun god, for example. The people being sacrificed were led to believe that their deaths were a privilege that would mean that the god would be pleased and allow them to spend eternity in some kind of heaven. You know it's not so different from the suicide bombers that we have today but, unfortunately, they kill other innocent people at the same time as they sacrifice themselves.'

'What about the Incas?' I asked, 'you know the Machu Picchu ones.'

'Well they were later and also not in the same place. They were mainly in Peru but the others were in Mexico and countries to the south like Bolivia and Guatemala.'

This discussion went on for some time until I realised that, interesting though it was, it was not helping with my geography homework so I left them to it. Looking at Daisy's face I could have predicted the subject of her next story.

'This is a story about looking for the Mayans in South America,' Daisy started, 'they were a tribe of people who lived there long ago and if you want to know more about them, ask Grandpa.'

My guess had been correct. I looked across and he gave me a big wink. I looked around as people shuffled to get comfortable before she began. Space for sitting was limited because Daisy's fame had spread and now our numbers were swelled by several neighbours and friends, all keen to listen to Grandpa John Willy's story.

Then, something unexpected: 'I think we should have a different story teller today,' Daisy smiled and crooked her finger at Grandpa.

The old man looked at her, surprised. 'Daisy, what are you doing?'

'I think everyone should know that this story is a joint effort. I needed some information about the history of the Mayans so Grandpa had to give me some advice and, in fact, wrote most of this with just a little help from me. So I think people would like it if he read the story, what do you think?' There was a general murmur of approval.

At first Grandpa shook his head. 'No, no, Daisy's the reader.'

But my sister was not to be denied. She stood and then threaded her way through the chairs, holding the typed pages towards him. With all eyes focused on him, Grandpa looked a bit embarrassed then, albeit reluctantly, he took the papers from Daisy and, in his deep, time worn tones, began to read.

'MAYA

'Lamania means submerged crocodile,' the guide, his boredom showing in his monotone delivery, intoned a clearly, well rehearsed monologue.

'There is some dispute about this name but you will see many crocodile carvings that suggest the importance of these animals in the life of this society. The ancient Maya had many gods to whom they sacrificed by bloodletting and by taking off the heads of captives. They had a belief that the world consisted of above and below earth. After death they thought that the soul would enter the underworld which was called Shee Bal Bah. This was a frightening place where sinister gods tested the dead souls. They had many gods; one called Chaac who was the god of thunder and rain he is depicted with a large nose. There was Ixtab who was the suicide goddess and Ixchel who was the rainbow goddess. She was believed to be the lover of the most important sun god called Kinich Ahau. He had the face of a jaguar with pointed teeth.'

Barbara was frantically writing all this information in her notebook so as to remember the strange names but she paused for a moment to ask, 'when did the people leave this area?'

She and Walter were interested in the history of the Mayan people but had done little pre-research. They regarded their holiday as a way of discovering more about South America generally rather than learning about the Maya specifically but, as the tour took in more of sites like Lamania they had become increasingly fascinated by these mysterious people who had built such amazing pyramids and temples, some of them, like this one, hidden in dense jungle.

Harry, probably not his real name, for he was clearly South American, looked irritated, he didn't care for questions that interrupted his flow. He had a script and wanted to get through this before these ignorant tourists asked banal questions. He thought that he had made this clear in the early part of the tour but a few people wouldn't follow his rule, notably Walter and Barbara, who were constantly questioning him during his delivery. Harry had begun to feel that they were doing this deliberately to annoy him so his answers were becoming increasingly brusque: 'five hundred BC to 1675, they lived here,' he growled.

Barbara had experienced his rudeness before and decided that it must be a way of covering his shyness. Surely guides rely on getting substantial tips from tourists and would be foolish to offend their customers, she reasoned, so she pursued her question:

'Why did they leave here?' She wondered, 'it's such a beautiful place.'

Now Harry was bordering on anger, largely because he didn't know the answer. 'We are still researching this,' he muttered.

'There must have been something,' Walter decided to join in. 'Maybe there was a flood, we're close to the river, or maybe the Spanish drove the people out.'

Harry's annoyance showed: 'you two

seem to have all the answers, maybe you should be the guides.' He spoke in such raised tones that members of the group were startled. Walter, usually a calm polite man, but having previously been aware of the guide's lack of respect, decided that he'd had enough.

'Right young man,' he said quietly, 'since you don't have the answers to our questions, I think we'll look around by ourselves and meet you back at the boat. What time shall we be leaving?'

Harry was a bit taken aback by this, looking rather embarrassed he looked at his watch and spoke in a sharp tone, 'it is better if you stay with me but, as you wish, we leave at seventeen hundred. Please don't be late, we have to go back up the river before our drive to the next hotel,' he added, now looking slightly deflated, maybe realising that he had allowed his annoyance to show.

'Right,' said Walter and, taking Barbara by the arm, walked away towards the nearest pyramid. Several others of the group looked hesitant wondering whether to join them but no-one moved, perhaps not feeling brave enough to wander around this unfamiliar place without a guide.

Barbara put her arm through Walter's, 'you're cross,' she said, 'you shouldn't let him annoy you; we've still got three more days with him while we're in Belize.'

'Maybe not,' Walter replied, 'I'm going to have a word with the Tour Leader, we need a better guide who knows his stuff and isn't going to be disrespectful to his charges. But, don't let this spoil our visit, it's a beautiful place and we can get a real feel for the atmosphere if we walk by ourselves.' He smiled reassuringly at his wife and put his arm round her as they proceeded to wander amongst the ruins.

The temple structure they were inspecting had an enormous face, like a mask, carved in the lower stones and, further along, was what appeared to be a small cell-like room with carved openings that may have been intended to represent the head of an animal, possibly a jaguar.

'Let's climb to the top,' Walter suggested.

'Do you think we should?' Barbara was wary. The rest of their group had disappeared into the jungle and they were now quite alone.

'It'll be fine, we've plenty of time and there should be some great shots over the jungle canopy.'

Walter was a keen photographer, sometimes to the point of obsession. Despite her misgivings, Barbara agreed, also keen to see the view from the top of the pyramid-like structure. The climb was not too steep and, by occasionally hanging on to one another, they easily managed the ascent. At the top they felt that their efforts had been rewarded, the view was magnificent, the air was fresher and the pesky mosquitoes had been left behind. The canopy stretched in a seemingly unending panorama towards the distant horizon. There were a few flashes of light that marked the river down which their motor boat had come but, otherwise all they could see was a patchwork of varying greens. A group of spider monkeys chattered and chased in some trees nearby and they heard the calls of several birds, with the occasional flash of colour revealing their whereabouts as they flitted through the trees.

Walter was already peering through the lens of his camera.

'Look over there,' he pointed at what appeared to be the top of a tall structure raising its head above the trees. 'Is that another pyramid do you think?'

Barbara looked in the direction he was pointing. She saw the irregular pile of grey-black stones he had seen and felt a shudder run down her back.

'It looks weird,' she answered, 'a bit threatening somehow.'

'Yes, a bit mysterious. How far do you think it is?'

Barbara knew immediately what he was planning. 'We've got to be back by five pm you know, we haven't got time to wander around a jungle.'

'Oh, we're alright,' Walter smiled at her trepidation, 'we've got two hours and if we follow the bearing from my compass, I guess we can be there and back in an hour. Come on love, let's give it a try, we can always turn back if it gets too late.'

Reluctantly, Barbara agreed. They clambered down the side of the pyramid and, using the compass bearing, set off in what they believed was the right direction.

Following a compass bearing is relatively straight forward on Yorkshire moorland but a South American forest is a different matter; dense undergrowth, streams and huge, buttressed tree trunks mean changes of direction are needed. Consequently, the walk took longer than the half hour allotted but despite their winding path, they reached what they decided was the structure they had seen reaching above the canopy.

This one was different, rather than a straight pyramid shape, it was built in huge steps too difficult for them to climb and, in the lower wall, rather than the small cell-like spaces on the other structure, this one appeared to have a bigger interior space that could be accessed by an entrance about three metres square.

Walter glanced at his watch, 'plenty of time, let's have a look inside.'

Despite her initial misgivings, Barbara couldn't resist the chance to discover what lay inside this beautiful and mysterious structure. Holding hands the two stepped out of the stifling heat of the jungle into the dark interior.

'Gosh it's cold,' the change in temperature was a shock, causing Walter to gasp.

'I can't see. Have you got the torch?' Barbara stood quite still holding tight to Walter's hand. He pulled the torch out of his rucksack and shone its beam towards the walls of a huge open space.

As the torch light penetrated the gloom, both of them emitted audible sighs. Unlike the outside walls which were the colour of weathered stone, the inside of the pyramid was full of colour. Before them they saw stylised designs of brightly coloured, exotic birds, forest trees with enormous buttress roots and animal figures that were recognisable as the jaguars, monkeys and the beautiful coati mundis that were found in this environment. Everything, plant or animal was painted in bright primary colours. The whole scene was such a shock that it was almost frightening.

Walter turned the torch slowly upwards and it was then that they realised that they were not looking at the interior walls of the pyramid but at a structure within a structure. Before them stood another pyramid, contained within the one whose walls they had just entered, but this one was not weathered with tiny patches of discoloured paint on the walls, it looked new as though it had only recently been created. The stones were cut with extraordinary precision to fit exactly together and the painting could have been completed yesterday. At each corner was a relief carving of a human head but their proportions were elongated as though the upper part the head had been squeezed and the eyes were crossed.

After several minutes, Walter and Barbara realised that they had been standing in silence both of them with their mouths slightly open. This was such an unexpected turn of events. It was as though they had been rendered dumb by the shock.

Walter recovered first. 'Why aren't the others here? Why didn't Harry bring us all to see this? It's just amazing and better than anything we've seen so far on this trip, everyone should see this… I'll take some photos to show them and bring them back here to see it.'

Barbara thought that Harry might have been keeping this for another day but Walter pointed out that this was their last day staying at their hotel, tomorrow they were supposed to travel on to somewhere else in Guatemala.

'He clearly had no intention of letting us see this for some reason,' he said crossly. 'Anyway I'd better take some pictures or we'll be late back.'

Pulling his camera and tripod out of the rucksack, he began to take the photographs, slowly moving round the walls of the structure to ensure that everything was recorded. Barbara followed entranced by the breathtaking decorations.

Too intent on his work as he walked round the side of the pyramid, Walter failed to see the waist high stone and, stepping sideways, bumped into it hurting his thigh. He cried with pain and looking round realised that there was actually a row of maybe six of these stones. His torch revealed that they were all the same height with elaborately carved sides and grooves cut in the flat, top surface. He focused on the grooves to see if they were depicting anything but could only see that they contained a reddish brown colouring.

Barbara arrived to discover why he had cried out and found him examining the stone blocks.

'What do you think of these?' He asked,

his pain forgotten. 'Look at this colour.'

Barbara bent forward and examined the grooves. She stepped back quickly.

'Oh Walter, don't you remember what Harry said? The Mayans indulged in human sacrifice. I think these are like the stones we saw in Mexico, where people's heads were cut off. That brown colour must be bl ... but it can't be it wouldn't still be here after all these years, would it?'

Before Walter could answer he was interrupted by a weird rustling noise and a powerful voice that seemed to fill the whole space with strange guttural sounds. They turned towards the voice and their torch revealed what seemed to be a male human figure completely covered by an elaborate costume clearly intended to represent a bird. The rustling sound was produced by a complex arrangement of huge, brightly coloured feathers that adorned the person's body. The arms were wings and the head was encased in a mask in the shape of the head of a large bird with an enormous hooked beak.

To say that the spectre was frightening would be an understatement. Barbara reached instinctively for Walter and he in turn wrapped his arms round her automatically offering protection. The strange guttural language was coming from this 'bird' and it continued to shout at them incomprehensibly waving its 'wings' which provided an unnerving background rattle.

'We er, we don't understand ...' Walter tried speaking back but this just seemed to infuriate the creature as it advanced threateningly but at least the shouting stopped. Then the bird-man suddenly paused in its advance and appeared to be thinking. Turning its back on the couple, it gave a strange cry. In the beam of torch light, another figure emerged, this one dressed in a long costume made from green material, apparently covered in scales which was so tight that the 'creature' had difficulty in moving. This new figure's head was hidden by a weird mask that seemed to represent a very old man with the head of a snake. Pointed fangs issued from his jaws but most alarming, he carried an axe.

'Oh, Walter, who are they, what are they doing here? I'm scared.'

Walter held his wife more tightly. 'I don't know love, let's just try to walk out, it might be the locals having a joke on the tourists. Just smile and stay close to me.'

The last instruction was superfluous since Barbara had no intention of leaving his side. They started to move towards the entrance which unfortunately was behind the creatures, only to find their way barred by a third apparition. This one had the appearance of a female with a tortured white face and a rope hanging from her neck. She shrieked incomprehensibly at the couple who stopped their advance and returned to their previous position, their backs unnervingly close to the blood stained stones.

Barbara began to sob uncontrollably which filled Walter with a sudden anger.

'Enough of this,' he shouted, 'who are

you, what do you want, you're frightening my wife.'

The creatures seemed unperturbed by his outburst and began to communicate with one another in the same strange language. It was almost as though they were oblivious to Walter and Barbara's presence.

Through her tears, Barbara whispered, 'they're in some kind of trance, do you think they're on drugs?' Before Walter could answer, a fourth figure emerged from the depths of the temple as if generated by the weird language of the other three. This one had the form of a male person but his body was skeletal, topped by a skull-like head. As he moved a necklace of bones dangling from his neck rattled, making a noise not unlike primitive wind chimes. He had the most threatening appearance of the whole group. Barbara began to sob uncontrollably now, turning her head away and clinging even more tightly to Walter who himself was soaked in a sweat caused by a combination of oppressive tropical heat and extreme tension. He was seriously worried that these creatures intended them harm and couldn't get out of his mind the sacrificial blocks that were so close behind them. Desperate for escape from this nightmare, he turned the fading beam of his torch to the floor, seeking for anything that could serve as a weapon. All he could see was a stone about the size of a cricket ball but with jagged edges. Thinking that he might be able to do some damage with this, he whispered to Barbara who bent with him as he picked it up.

As they regained their position, they

were surprised to find that a fifth figure now stood with the others. This one had no costume apart from a simple covering for his lower body. There was congealed blood on his forehead, he had bruising around very muscular legs and his hands were tied behind his back but despite this he stood tall and straight with a proud demeanour. Now the group of strangely dressed figures gathered around a stone block that the couple had not noticed before and the skeletal creature motioned the captive towards it. Without resisting the poor creature knelt and placed his head on the block.

The guttural shouting now became more rhythmic, almost like a primitive prayer.

'What are they doing … are they going to…? The remainder of Barbara's sentence dried in her throat as the snake-like creature raised his axe and, with apparent ease, severed the prisoner's head from his body. Instantly, blood flowed freely down the sides of the block and the horrifying object fell to the floor, while the captive's body slumped, twitching behind the sacrificial block.

Barbara let out a wail of despair and her body went slack by Walter's side. Something within, whether it was a rush of adrenaline or an internal mechanism for survival allowed him to act. Realising the immediate need to escape, he grabbed his wife's limp body, raised her in his arms and ran towards the entrance that he knew was behind the executioners, intending, by sheer weight of desperation to force his way through. The nearest was the bird figure, driving straight towards it, he expected to collide with a mass of feathers and hopefully knock it out of the way. But the impact did not occur; he seemed instead to pass straight through which caused him to stagger and almost fall as he had prepared himself to meet with significant resistance. Just recovering his balance and finding strength beyond his expectation, Walter rushed through the space and out into sweltering forest.

As his strength finally failed, he fell on to a grass covered rise, instinctively spinning so that Barbara's body fell against his. He looked behind expecting a chase but nothing ...no running figures, no cries of anger just a faint light from the entrance which almost immediately faded away.

Too exhausted to move, Walter lay on the ground waiting to recover his breath, intending to continue his escape as soon as his strength had returned. Barbara, still in a faint, moaned and cried out but her words made no sense except to express the fear she had felt inside the temple. Walter leaned over and spoke quietly: 'don't worry love I don't think they're following us, just rest a while and then we'll try to find the way back to the river.'

His words seemed to bring his wife out of her faint. She opened her eyes and glanced fearfully around, 'what happened?' She asked, anxiously.

'I'm not sure. You fainted when they ...'

'Oh, I remember, they chopped his head off, that poor man ... I thought we were next ... then it went black, I was so scared.'

'I know you were. I picked you up and just ran, they didn't stop me and no-one has followed us. I just don't understand it. They were dressed like the gods that Harry talked about. It was like a dream but we were awake.'

'Oh, Walter, let's just get out of here, they might still come after us.'

Barbara stood – a bit unsteady on her feet - but ready to run if necessary. Walter was about to begin walking with her when the sound of people approaching through the forest made the hairs on the back of his neck stand up.

'They're coming,' Barbara almost screamed as Harry, leading the rest of the group, appeared at the end of a narrow track coming out of the undergrowth. As usual, he was talking: 'now this is a special reconstruction of a Mayan temple. They used to build new temples on top of older ones so you see the newer temple and then we'll go inside to see a reconstructed older one but it has been painted in exactly the way that they would have done it. We shall also see a show that has been created using light projection of computer generated images of the gods, Kinich Ahau a sun god who took the form of a macaw, Chaac who looks like a snake and is the god of rain and thunder, Ixtab who is the suicide goddess and most frightening, Yum Cimil, the death god. You can tell him, he's covered with bones but I must warn you that when he arrives, something quite shocking happens and …' His voice tailed off as he saw Walter and Barbara staring at him. 'Oh, hello, you've beaten us to it, have you been inside?''

This time it was Mum who spoke first, 'Oh, I'm so relieved, I thought it was real, those poor people, they must have been so frightened.' Her voice broke the silence that had accompanied the telling of the story and people started to talk to one another until Dad called order: 'we need to thank these two, I thought that was a great story, well done both of you.' There was a short round of hesitant yet genuine applause and then everyone started talking again.

A few days later, Grandpa asked if we would get together in the 'reading room', as he had an announcement. Dutifully we arrived at the appointed time wondering what he had in mind.

'Well folks, I've decided to stay alive for a bit longer and it's all down to Daisy. I've enjoyed listening with you all to her stories but most interesting was when we worked together on the last one. I've talked with her and she has agreed that we can do some more for the family but I've also thought that I could actually write a book about my travels and er ... maybe,' his voice went quite, 'maybe, try to get it published,' he finished somewhat bashfully.

'Great idea Grandpa,' Christine said and walked over and cuddled him. He looked pleased and I knew why, Christine gives good cuddles.

'Yes and well done Daisy,' Dad spoke

looking round for his daughter but she had gone. 'Where's Daisy?' he asked

Mum knew, 'She's gone to her room, I think she had an idea for a story.'

A week of school, homework and everyday events for the family passed quickly. Without any discussion as to whether or not things would be the same as usual, the family and a few friends gathered on Saturday evening in what had become known as 'the story room'. We waited expectantly hoping that we were not to be disappointed. We need not have worried because we were about to hear Grandpa's first story! He made a grand entrance with Daisy holding his arm. They bowed ceremoniously to everyone and then Daisy announced, 'welcome to Grandpa's first solo story. He has written it totally by himself and he hopes you will like it. I've heard it and it's great.' This last part she said with a threatening glance which effectively dared anyone to find criticism.

'Thank you mademoiselle for your kind introduction,' said John Willy formally, 'she is of course too kind and I know you will appreciate that she is a hard act to follow but, nevertheless, hope that you will find some morsel of enjoyment from my poor offering.' This said, he lowered himself, with a slight groan, into the story chair and we quietened down with anticipation. The old man gathered his papers together, moved his spectacles to the end of his nose and began:-

'It's called **WALKABOUT**

Some of you will know that I spent some time wandering in Australia. People there call it 'going walkabout'. It is a large Country with some huge areas of land where only a few people live and most of these are aboriginals who live natural lives along with some of the strange animals that inhabit the bush. They understand the wild country and are able to find food and water in the most unpromising environment. The climate was challenging for me, very hot and dry most of the time and what I was doing was very foolish and could easily have resulted in my death from starvation, thirst or both. I had actually gone there to work on a sheep station, which I thought would be different and interesting but the boss was a bully who treated his crew badly and I'm afraid that for some reason he decided that I would be his whipping boy. He called me 'that stupid pommie' and gave me all the unpleasant jobs to do. He made my life unbearable until I decided that I couldn't stay there any longer. The problem was that the nearest town, where I might find another job, was many miles away and it was only a very small settlement, so leaving meant covering long distances with the possibility of no work when I arrived.

The sheep station was near a place called Mamungari in South Australia and I knew that if I could manage to head in an easterly direction, I could reach a strange town called Coober Pedy. One of the sheep shearers had told me, that people there look for opals under the ground, which they then sell, sometimes for good money. In fact, particularly fine examples were worth a small fortune. He also told me that many people there live underground because of the heat so it could be a good place for a pale faced Englishman who couldn't stand the hot sun. I had made friends with the cook who secretly put together a package of food, a heavy but necessary bottle of water, a coffee pot and a tiny frying pan. He warned me not to let anyone know or he himself might feel the boss's wrath.

So I launched myself innocently on to what was to become an arduous journey, with only a heavy rucksack of food and water and a canvas bag laughingly termed a 'one man tent'. I knew there were dangerous animals in the outback, particularly spiders, so I determined not to sleep in the open.

At first I felt light and optimistic, happy to be away from the oppressive atmosphere of the sheep station. My step was light and I had in my head a tune the shearers sang as they relieved the sheep of their woollen fleeces. Having thoroughly studied a map of my intended journey, I was relying on my old compass to provide the correct bearing that should bring me close to my intended destination.

On that first day I walked until the sun got close to the horizon and then quickly sought some shelter where I might settle down for the night. A group of stunted gum trees formed a rudimentary circle within which I could raise my 'tent'. I heated some soup which I ate with a chunk of the bread provided by the cook and, feeling very tired, lay in my tent with just my head outside so that I could observe the night sky and listen to the sounds of the desert.

I slept badly. Even though the bush is a barren place where few animals live, they still manage to fill the night with strange noises, some of which sounded like the cries of lost souls. There were alarming rustles and scuttles suggesting a night time fight for survival. I also couldn't avoid the thought that a funnel-web spider might be creeping unnoticed into my tiny tent to feast upon my naked flesh. My small fire soon died out causing me to snuggle down into my cover away from the chill of the desert night.

I must have slept for a while because I woke with a start, wondering why the sheep station was so quiet. Usually I wake to bleating, the sound of male voices, cursing and coughing, along with dogs barking and the smell of Cooky's breakfast preparations. For a moment I missed the busyness and wondered whether it might be better to retrace my steps and ask for my job back. I quickly dismissed the thought, knowing that I would not be welcomed, particularly by the boss and determined to continue my journey.

I relit my small fire and managed to cook a passable breakfast of eggs and bacon using the little frying pan. I had forgotten to acquire some sugar so the coffee was too bitter for my taste.

The morning was clear and bright and, initially, a fine temperature for walking. Feeling more optimistic now, I gathered my goods together and, glancing at my compass, set off towards some distant hills that appeared to be in the correct direction. Progress was slow for, although the terrain looked fairly flat, there were hidden hollows and rises along with some sections of impenetrable bush that made walking difficult. Also, the sun rose quickly into a clear blue sky and I was soon breathing heavily and thinking about seeking some shade where I might spend the middle hours of the day. I kept glancing into the distance, trying to make sure that I was still heading towards the hills but hot air from the desert floor was rising in a rippling motion that twisted distant features out of shape. Nevertheless, I was pretty sure that my course had not deviated.

As night fell on my second day, the isolation began to envelop me. Now I felt very alone. While I had tried to keep a straight path there was little likelihood, even if I turned back immediately, that I would be able to find my way. The stupidity of launching myself into the outback with little previous experience came home to me but there was little else I could do. A strange kind of resignation established itself in my mind: I must carry on and if I made it, good and if I died trying, then so be it. Whether I was affected by the heat and glare of the sun or by feelings of great fatigue I'm not sure but my dread of isolation was replaced by feelings of great calm.

The second night was much like the first except that this time I slept through the night noises and awoke feeling more refreshed but with a raging thirst. The thought of eggs and bacon made me feel nauseous so I simply took a deep swig from my precious water supply, which by now was so warm that it could hardly be distinguished from the temperature of the air. I was beginning to feel grubby and thought about having a shave but could not sacrifice my precious water supply for such a luxury. I simply collected my meagre belongings together and set off along the compass bearing of the previous day.

Three more days and nights passed in much the same way as I penetrated deeper into unknown country. I used my supplies as carefully as possible and tried to find shade when the sun was at its highest. My legs seemed to be coping well and a crude parasol made from a shirt fastened with spare bootlaces to an appropriately shaped thin, tree branch served to provide some shade. My determination to survive was still strong, although I had abandoned the notion of reaching Coober Pedy and replaced if with the more achievable goal of reaching any kind of settlement in which I might find some way to make a living.

After these five days, however, I was very aware of the need to find a source of water. As I had seen in films about the aborigines, I tried digging a hole in the desert to see if water would flow but whether I wasn't going deep enough or not selecting a suitable place to excavate, I don't know but I simply made myself exhausted and hot. Feelings of resignation began to creep in: maybe I would die here; I could imagine my bones sticking out of the sand for some weary traveller to find and think, 'I wonder who this poor soul was?'

Preoccupied with these gloomy thoughts, I almost fell down a steep slope as I came upon it unexpectedly. Managing to keep upright, I was surprised to find myself looking down into a deep, hollow area with a crumbly slope of red rocks and sand in front of me. At the bottom of the slope was an extraordinary pool of what seemed like clear, deep water, on the other side of which was a rocky cliff about twenty metres high. To say that it looked inviting, would be an understatement, I could barely contain my impulse to run down the slope and fling myself into the cool depths.

I scrambled down, trying not to fall, until I reached a fairly flat area beside the pool. Unable to resist further, I took off my boots and clothes, threw my rucksack aside and allowed myself the luxury of stepping into the cool water. The bank was very steep and I was soon out of my depth. I swam slowly to the centre of the pool and then turned on my back and floated, gazing up into a cloudless sky, allowing the luxury of cool water to ease my aching limbs. Strangely, a song from my childhood came into my mind and I thought longingly of the cool air and green fields of England. My eyes wandered along the cliff top. As my view approached the sun I blinked to avoid the glare. I knew that the power of the rays could destroy my vision. The ancient wall of rock seemed to bend towards me as though it was about to fall. A green bird shrieked a warning and I then saw him.

A figure, here in the desolation of the outback, a man who seemed to know me, looked down. I couldn't see his face clearly; his eyes were just dark shadows. I could discern the shape of a long stout stick by his side but I didn't feel threatened. I guessed that he might be an aborigine, since they were the only people likely to be wandering around here, although I wasn't sure where 'here' was.

I let my legs drop below the surface so as to release my arm to wave to him. In my haste, I managed to sink and took a mouthful of water. By the time I had recovered from semi-choking myself, he had disappeared. Now I wondered if he had really been there or was it just the silhouette of the dead tree that teetered on the edge of the cliff. In any case, if he had been real, he had gone away and I was enjoying the water too much to bother about him.

I continued to float lazily until my limbs actually began to feel a little cold and I was quite hungry. I wondered if there were any fish in the pool, it was certainly deep enough and the thought of supplementing my diet with some fresh fish caused my juices to run. I looked round and found a suitable branch to make a rod; some cotton intended for repairs made a fine enough line and a witchetty grub poked out of a rotting tree made useful bait. I collected a few more of these creatures, knowing that in themselves they were good to eat. Casting my line and allowing the weight of the fat grub to take it under water, I settled down, hoping for bite. I had no hook but thought that a fish would hardly be able to swallow such a big grub before I had pulled it out.

I waited, trying to sit quite still so as not to frighten away a nervous barramundi. Nothing – not the wobble of a single fin occurred, let alone a bite. After about half an hour, I jammed the rod between some rocks and lay back feeling very weary…

'You will have no success with such a feeble method.'

I awoke with a start. The voice seemed close to my ear. I looked around but, at first, could see no-one. Then I raised my chin and looked behind to find a face looking down on me from above.

'Crayfish meat is best, they don't like the witchetty. Look under stones in the water for crayfish.'

He was burned almost black by the sun and his hair had been bleached till it was nearly white and, if this was the man I had seen earlier, he was not a native aborigine but unmistakably an oriental maybe a Chinaman. The sun had dropped towards the horizon so I must have been asleep for at least an hour. How long had he been there? I scrambled to achieve a more suitable posture for receiving a guest, feeling vulnerable lying on the ground.

I got to my feet and, not really knowing what to say, simply held out my hand.

'Hello, I'm John Willy, I think I'm lost.' Was all that I could think of to say.

He smiled, revealing very white teeth. Shaking my hand, he spoke in a curiously rhythmic voice, 'Hello, John Willy, I am called Michael. I am not lost.'

His handshake was firm and the look in his eyes suggested that he was friendly. 'I wonder why you are here, are you looking for something or maybe someone? Perhaps I can help you.'

Not wishing to reveal my foolishness in running away from the sheep station with only an embryonic plan, I just said that I was going walkabout, which seems to be generally acceptable hereabouts.

'Ah, I see,' Michael replied 'I thought you might be an opal hunter. Many people, usually men, come by here looking for these stones, thinking they will make themselves rich but only a few are successful.'

He was dressed strangely for the outback. He wore a long, loose fitting garment that covered most of his body. It was basically cream coloured but covered with elaborate embroidery in the shapes of dragons with long twisting tails and beautiful stylised birds of paradise. It seemed far too delicate to wear in countryside where spines, scrub and thorns were likely to reduce it to shreds. But, although my eyes took in the nature of the garment, they were drawn to something far more extraordinary; certainly, the long gold chain round his neck caught my gaze but it was the pendant swinging loosely at the end that I could not ignore. Encased in a golden frame was the most exquisite opal that I had ever seen.

I made little effort to ignore the gem and found myself gazing at it as though hypnotised.

I could not have described its dominant colour. As it swung with Michael's movement, it changed from pale yellow to rich purple. There were highlights of silver but at its heart was a glow of the most extraordinary, deep red I had ever seen. It seemed to burn with an unquenchable, inner fire, which flickered then danced, faded, then glowed again. The stone had unfathomable depth. It was as though a man could drown in it, engulfed by its endless beauty.

I am ashamed to say that I immediately desired this stone from the centre of my being. To hold it and gaze at it for eternity seemed the answer to all my needs. Hunger and thirst were gone, possession was paramount. It had to be mine.

Involuntarily, I reached forward to touch but it swayed out of my reach. Gently, Michael put his hand on mine. 'Ah, you see this. Is it not beautiful?'

I forced myself to look away and into his face. It was a face of ultimate kindness. 'It is indeed an amazing stone but, sad to say, it is cursed. I wear it for all my days. This is the burden I must bear for my great sin.'

He smiled as he spoke but I could sense an extreme sadness behind the smile. Unable to resist, I was about to ask him to explain but, before I could speak, he raised his hand to prevent my words. 'Do not ask my friend because I could never tell you what I did, I am too ashamed. The stone weaves spells and makes us mad with longing. Please remove it from your mind. Come, let us walk I have food and shelter which you are welcome to share.'

He led me around the back of the pool using a pathway that I had not previously noticed to a dark shadow in the cliff face which turned out to be a small cave. He indicated that I should enter and as my eyes became accustomed to the darkness, I was surprised by its depth. A small oil lamp, hanging from the roof, glowed dimly until he turned up the wick to create more light, revealing two chairs set against a wooden table which was covered with an exquisitely embroidered cloth upon which were two tin cups and plates as if waiting for us to arrive. Further back in the cave, I could make out some stone shelves carved into the wall, containing cooking utensils and oriental jars which I imagined might contain spices or other foods. Nearby was a stove holding a large cooking pot full of rice, which simmered gently. In the darker recesses of the room I could just make out two camp beds with a woollen rug placed between.

'You see, I was expecting a visitor, after I saw you swimming in the pool,' he smiled, indicating the table and the cooking pot.

'But, er ... do you live here?' Was all I could think to say, wondering how it could be that this strange and charming man appeared to have a home in this isolated place.

'Oh yes, this is my home. I must live here for all my life.' He smiled again as though there was nothing unusual about his situation.

Before I could ask more questions, he waved to one of the chairs, 'come sit, I will prepare food, you must be hungry, I cannot let a guest go without food.'

I instantly became aware of an extreme hunger and feelings of fatigue. I slumped into one of the chairs, while my host took away the plates and started spooning rice from the large pot and adding other ingredients from the jars on the shelves. Before long he placed before me a plate of steaming rice with added vegetables and some kind of meat saying, 'you can try the crayfish, they are themselves good to eat. I have some rice wine also, would you like to try it?'

In my hunger, I had already started to spoon food into my mouth so I could only manage a weak smile and a nod to indicate my agreement. Soon my mouth was filled with extraordinary flavours. The food was delicious; the best I had ever tasted and the wine provided a superb accompaniment. My plate was soon empty but he instantly provided more, without questioning my need. As my stomach began to fill, I noticed that he was not eating but before I could ask, he answered, 'I am not hungry my friend but I enjoy your appetite, please eat your fill.'

Eventually, I could eat no more and sat back in my seat. With his perpetual smile, he invited me to accept a small dumpling.

'You will enjoy this it is sweet dim sum, it will touch your heart,' he said as his smile turned into a laugh.

Unable to resist I ate the sweet confection and it was truly a fine epilogue to a superb meal.

After some quiet conversation during which he told me that he had lived quite comfortably in this cave for several years, I thanked my host profusely and rose to leave. Quickly he stepped in front of me with his arms raised, preventing my departure. For a moment I felt threatened but this passed as he smiled again.

'Please, do not think of leaving, it is getting dark and there is a comfortable bed here. You are welcome to stay.'

In truth, I felt a mixture of exhaustion and contentment and had no difficulty in accepting his suggestion, even though it seemed more like an order than an invitation. I muttered my thanks and without even considering that my actions might be considered ill-mannered, slumped onto the camp bed and fell instantly into a deep and dreamless sleep.

How many hours passed I could not say but I awoke with a start, wondering where I was and worried that I might have overslept and be in for trouble with the boss. It was with some relief that, through the dim light of the oil lamp, I made out the walls of the cave. I looked across to the other bed where my host slept peacefully, his breathing a steady rhythm.

Something glowed by his bed; the opal on its gold chain, although still fastened round his neck, hung down, almost touching the ground. Even from the other side of the cave I felt its attraction. It seemed almost to be calling, 'I can be yours, take me, see my beauty, live in my light.' I was again filled with a lust for this extraordinary thing.

I wondered what crime he might have committed for the stone. Maybe if he stole it, I could take it because it wasn't really his, he didn't deserve it. In my befuddled state, I even convinced myself that I might return it to its rightful owner. He seemed sound asleep. Perhaps I could sneak over there and remove it from his neck, just to look at it more closely ... only to look, to hold ...

I was by his bed. Even in sleep he seemed to be smiling. I reached to touch the opal. It burned in my hand, almost too hot to hold. But now it was mine, it belonged to me, I must take it from him. His trust and friendship meant nothing. I must tear this thing from his neck. I tried to lift it from his neck but it was impossible, it was trapped behind his head. I wondered if I might break the slender chain. I pulled carefully and then harder and harder as he remained asleep. Surely he will wake. I dared to pull harder. Suddenly it came away but strangely did not break. Instead the chain wrapped round my neck. I felt the heat of the opal against my bare skin. It was on me, it was mine but the joy I had expected was missing. I could scarcely breathe. I tried to lift it over my head but it was impossible. It clung to me as a boa constrictor might. It had extraordinary power I did not own the opal, it owned me, I was powerless to resist.

'Ah, now you know what I did,' Michael looked at me but with a scornful gaze rather than his usual smile. 'I too stole the opal but it is not a jewel, it is a monster. It will keep you here for all your life unless you can find some greedy fool such as yourself. That will be your only escape. What we saw was only a mirage. The pool does not exist. There is no food for you now. For you there is nothing. Now you may understand why I could not eat with you. But for me now there is freedom. At last I can leave this awful place where no man comes.'

He smiled but it was a smile of triumph not friendship. Michael walked quickly to the cave entrance and disappeared. I ran to stop him but he was gone. Outside, in the burning heat, there was no water, inside, no lamp, no furniture, no stove or jars, no steaming rice ... nothing but me alone with a crudely carved, hot stone round my neck. I looked down and saw that it no longer had the deep intense glow instead it was just a dull, ordinary piece of rock on a heavy, iron chain.'

Grandpa sat back, pulled his papers together and then looked round.

'Oh ... so you were left there in the desert but how did you get out?' I could never keep my mouth shut. I got so involved in the stories. A cushion bounced off my head.

'Idiot,' said Josh, 'it's a story, grandpa made it up, it's not real. You are a clown.'

'Leave him alone,' Grandpa defended me, 'he concentrates on the story, nothing wrong with that. It's a compliment really, means he was able to imagine what happened so clearly that he takes a while to get back to reality. What do you think I should call the story, Michael?'

I thought for a minute, ignoring Joshua's demands to 'get on with it.'

'How about 'walkabout'', I suggested.

'A fine title, Michael, that'll be it, well done,' Grandpa grinned.

Josh looked a bit sheepish, 'I liked it too Grandpa but I'm not such wuss as to think it's real.'

I was about to throw the cushion back when Mum intervened, telling us to stop before we caused some damage, 'it was a good tale Dad. You should write some more, it will give Daisy a rest. Now I need some help with the tea, anybody volunteer.'

'Me love,' said Dad. 'Michael, you and Josh can set the table and try not to argue.'

Dad made his special poached eggs with baked beans on toast and we had some of Mum's chocolate brownies with ice cream for afters. There was a lot of talk about the story, with everyone agreeing that it made them want to go and visit Australia. Grandpa said that it was a special place and if anyone went, he'd be willing to act as a guide. I saw Mum look at him strangely but she said nothing.

Afterwards, Josh and I said we'd go to the park with the football and other folk were beginning to move away from the dining table, when Grandpa spoke: 'before everyone goes, can I just say something?'

We stopped and waited for him to speak.

'I know I said I'd had enough of life and

I also know now how stupid and selfish I was. Well, I can only say that I'm very, very sorry for being an old idiot, particularly to my lovely daughter who I know was upset by my actions. The past few weeks have taught me something important. No matter how ill or fed up you feel, life in a family is a precious thing and I'm very lucky to be here with all of you. The fact that Daisy was willing to give up her time to write stories for a stupid old man showed me how much I have to be grateful for and, when we worked together on Mayan story, I realised how much I enjoyed remembering the places I had seen and bringing them back to life. So, I'm finished with my idea about living in the downstairs toilet. I've decided to write a book of stories about all the places I've been and see if I can get it published and, if people would like to hear them as I go along, we can have regular family meetings like now and maybe Daisy will have some more as well, what do you think?'

I looked at Mum and saw what I was expecting, her eyes were wet but a lovely smile lit her face. Dad spoke for us all. 'John Willy, we're all glad that you've changed your mind. We enjoy having you here with us and it's a great idea to write down your memories. I'm sure Daisy will always keep on making up stories, so we'll have good times like these for years to come.'

There was a general murmur of agreement. Daisy and Mum went and hugged John Willy and Josh and I set off for the park feeling good about our family and experiencing feelings of brotherly love, well almost …

Copyright © 2017 George Mitchell Cover design by Mitchybwoy. All rights reserved.

You might enjoy another book by George Mitchell, it's called 'Michael's War' and is available in both print and Kindle versions on Amazon

Printed in Poland
by Amazon Fulfillment
Poland Sp. z o.o., Wrocław